Please Swipe Again

MEGAN MANN

authorHOUSE®

AuthorHouse™
1663 Liberty Drive
Bloomington, IN 47403
www.authorhouse.com
Phone: 1-800-839-8640

First published by AuthorHouse 10/18/2010

ISBN: 978-1-4520-9310-9 (sc)
ISBN: 978-1-4520-9311-6 (e)

Library of Congress Control Number: 2010915392

Printed in the United States of America

This book is printed on acid-free paper.

Certain stock imagery © Thinkstock.

For Ben and Megan
Without either of you, this would still be a dream

CHAPTER ONE

Ava

My boyfriend is a piece of shit. Well, I guess you would consider him my ex-boyfriend now, but whatever the title, he's still a piece of shit. After three years of dating and roughly 102 miles between us, he calls to break up with me over the phone. Mind you, he was here just the day before and couldn't grow a pair to tell me in person that "it just wasn't working out anymore." Seriously, he did that over the phone. All I could think about after I hung up was, "Did he just Joe Jonas and Taylor Swift me?" I'll have to let him know when I find his balls in the bargain bin of a Wal-Mart so he can have them back, but that's highly unlikely.

Now that that waste of 17 minutes of my T-Mobile minutes is over, I'm just sitting here staring at a wall and unsure of what to do. Do I cry, do I throw something or do I just say "fuck it" and move on? I mean, there is some guy who has an entire philosophy on just looking at your problems and saying "fuck it," so that could work out to my benefit but that wouldn't solve anything, would it? No, I guess not.

I could cry, but where would that get me? As I ponder that shining gem of a possibility, I think back on all the times that I have cried in regards to him. I remember one time in particular, seeing as it was as recently as two

1

years ago. It was the day that we had to say good-bye as he went down to Indiana University and I was left to finish my last year of high school miles apart from each other. We said that we trusted each other and we knew that there was a lot of love going on, so we saw it as a "see you later" rather than an "I'm free at last!" sort of thing. I had a pretty stoic look going on until my mom and I were back on the highway and she had to pull over due to my tears that somewhat resembled convulsions. She told me it would be all A-OK. Did I believe her? Of course not. There's always that sinking feeling in your stomach that something is going to go wrong.

Of course it did.

Learn to always trust your gut. It's never going to let you down, and it didn't let me down this time. It didn't matter how hard I wished that what I was feeling was completely made up in my head. I knew that a turn in our smooth road of love was about to come up. When he came to see me, I felt like my ill feelings and thoughts were a pointless waste of my time. That is, until I heard "Wish You Were Here" blasting off of my phone and got that awesome line of, "This just isn't working out anymore. What do you want me to say?" At least think up a better line, Kyle. I mean, really.

While my brain did the noodle dance in an attempt to make sense of it all, I heard my phone ring. It was the general ringtone of Muse so I knew it wasn't Sir Suckalot, but I couldn't answer it. If I were to talk to anyone, I was bound to break down and tears just weren't in style yet. Maybe in 43 minutes, give or take 39 of those, they'd be in fashion, but not just yet. Maybe a little music would make me feel better. That never let me down whenever I needed a quick pick me up. It was the one aspect of my life that I knew would never turn its back on me or say that it didn't have time for me. I grabbed my iPod off of the docking station and searched around for my headphones. I flipped over pillows and looked near stacks of magazines and couldn't find them. Finally, I spotted them peeking out from beneath a pile of discarded clothes from the night before.

I plugged them in and hit shuffle as I paced the room. Though it was as if my iPod was somehow connected to my thought process, it started spitting out love song after love song after love song. Why does it always know when you're not wanting to listen to those songs but it plays them anyway? I heard all the ones you do not want to hear in a time like this.

"Your Body is a Wonderland" by John Mayer was skipped to "Dice" by Finley Quaye which was swapped for "Love Song" by 311 which turned into "Stay With You" by John Legend and so on with an array of Beatles songs splattered throughout. There was a good chance it had suddenly sprouted wings, because I don't think my iPod could have fluttered across the room any faster than it did.

I slid down to the floor and pulled my knees into my chest, letting my head fall back and land on the mattress of my bed. After letting out a large sigh, I started to really think about it. That wasn't something I had wanted to do, so I grabbed my tattered copy of *The Catcher In The Rye* and picked up where I had left off. As if the music was not enough, I realized that I had stopped at the point in the book where Holden was down in the bar of his hotel with the three girls at the table next to him. How is it possible that I landed on the paragraph where he describes how easy it is to fall in love with someone? In the hopes of finding out how fast a paperback could reach the other side of the room, the book took flight as well.

My only option was to go back and think of what had happened. The conversation just replayed itself in my head over and over as I tried to pinpoint the real reason.

"But you were just here yesterday," I said. "Why couldn't you have told me this YESTERDAY?" I said with my confusion and anger starting to rise.

"Well, I thought that it might be better to do this over the phone. I've been thinking and I'm pretty sure that we've run out of tokens for this game we've been playing. I'm here and you're there."

I thought about this for a second before I responded. He must have lost his marbles on the drive back from his visit 24 hours before. The surplus of questions just continued to increase every time he let silence fill the air. Possible reasons for this middle-school style break up began to cloud my brain before I could choke out, "How is this JUST NOW becoming a problem?" in a rather loud fashion.

He said, "Why are you yelling? I'm trying to calmly, honestly and reasonably talk to you about this."

Calmly? Why am I yelling? What does he expect from me? He's breaking up with me, not helping me bake cupcakes.

"Honesty? You don't even know what that is! You can't even tell me the real reason that you're thinking of breaking up with me or why you couldn't do it yesterday to my face!"

Silence. Great. Now is the time that he chooses to pipe down. After another few silent seconds, I decide to lower my voice and say what I'm really thinking.

"Did you just think that I would just grovel at your feet and beg you to reconsider? I feel like that's what you want me to do. It's not going to happen, just so we're clear. We should have broken up a long time ago. I bet it's not working anymore because you want to get with that other girl. Well, it's that or you already have."

Well, I was right to think he had gone behind my back. The last three months were spent with some trailer trash tramp who didn't care that he had a girlfriend that he'd met during the Maymester of summer school. At least, that's what I had gathered about her. I'm sure the slut has a really nice personality. Well, no, I'm sure she does not, but I thought I would at least try to be a little civil.

Finally, I gave way to my feelings and let the tears flow. Were they angry tears or the kind of tears only heartbreak can render? I wasn't sure. Either way, I was expecting a flow to the likes of Niagara Falls, but instead I was oddly greeted by just a small river. But then I really thought about it and something that had nothing to do with heartbreak and that stupid male crossed my mind. It was altogether different and had come from out of left field. I just wish I'd had a mitt to catch it instead of getting the wind knocked out of me.

When did I become so old? When was that lightning flash to my life that sent me from tiny tot to big girl? I've reached the point where if I leave the house, I check my hair in the mirror. I have to remember where I placed my keys and make sure I grabbed my phone. I don't even remember when I required enough junk to fill up the purse that can house a small infant.

From the time you can walk and talk, you voice your desire to be older. You say how you can't wait to reach your sweet sixteen and get to drive mommy's car. Perhaps you can't wait to be 18 when you have close to no limits on what you can do. The real kicker is when you go to tell them your age before the new R-rated film and 18 comes flying out. Suddenly bewildered, you stop to look around and wonder aloud, "Ew, am I really that old? Just yesterday I wanted a ride to the mall to shop at Limited Too after I finished my language arts workbook." It's even worse when all of a sudden you realize that you are almost to the point where you can walk right into a bar knowing that the age on your ID is now the legal limit.

Life is coming up on me fast. All I want to be is that naive little eight-year-old again daydreaming about life in the big city. I want to have limitless days and have no boundaries too fearful of crossing. I don't want days full of friends in drunken stupors trying to forget about heartbreak and failing classes. The vibrancy that life held has taken a back seat to all the pain of growing up. It's time to find it again.

We're so caught up and busy planning for what is going to happen next, that we don't stop and go, "Hot damn, what's going on right here and now?" We lose sight of what's important right now because we're more concerned with what will be important in the next five years. I mean, did it ever occur to anyone that I don't want to know what happens next? I want the element of surprise in my life, not a scheduled plan of when to eat, sleep and shit.

As my mind continued to spiral, the tears had stopped and the revelation came into mind. I need a break from small-town America to see what else is out there. Everywhere else seems so much more interesting, like everything really is happening where you aren't living life. I want that part of my life back where I just picked up and relocated myself for a week or two. What if I just got up and went? Who would stop me? I control my life. I make the decisions. This time, though, it would be just a little bit longer. A semester long, to be exact. Fate seemed to be on my side, because a second later, the answer came in the medium of a phone call.

Through sniffles I answered with a hello.

"Hey, are you sick? Why do you sound so congested?"

Madison was always straight to the point. We met nine years ago when her dad started to work with my parents at their law firm in Chicago. She was a few years older than me, but we got along when we met at the firm's Fourth of July barbecue that year. We bonded over our matching jelly sandals and talked about our preference for 'N Sync over Backstreet Boys, how we liked to stay up and watch Nick At Nite, and of course, boys. Over time, we managed to become best friends and relied on each other for everything.

When she moved to New York City to major in psychology, I felt a little bit like I was losing my partner in crime. Luckily, our friendship could withstand all those miles and make us feel like we were two minutes away.

I sighed, "You really know how to make a gal feel special, don't you? I guess I might as well tell you. Dick McGee just ended it." I heard her gasp and I continued. "And before that conversation even begins, no, I do not want to talk about it right now. It was literally ten minutes ago. That's not what's important, what's important is-" But I couldn't even get out what I was ready to say before she was already speaking.

"I always knew that he was a piece of shit. I'm sorry, I didn't want to say it, but he is," Madison said rather quickly. "So, what are you going to do? If you didn't yell at him yet, you have to do something. You can go up there and junk punch him! Yeah, that'd be good!" She seemed beside herself with the prospect with swift pain to the balls. Clearly, I needed to cut her off if I wanted to get anything said.

"MADISON!" I shouted.

She stopped. "Oh, I'm sorry. I seemed to have gotten carried away with myself. Okay, what is it you want to say? Wait, how did he do it?"

"I'm going to have to talk about this with you, aren't I?"

I could practically hear the smile she cracked on the other end. "Of course you are. I can't let my best friend keep this all inside. Now, how did he do it? Was it by ending the relationship tag on Facebook? That's obviously what means it's really over these days."

"You know, if you could see me, you'd see the intense eye roll I just threw at you. No, it was pretty classy, though. You know how I told you he was coming to visit? He acted like it was all rainbows and butterflies yesterday when he was here and then called me today to do it over the phone. Apparently he'd been seeing someone else. I sort of figured that he would go for that girl anyway."

"Which one? The one with the lazy eye?" she asked.

"No," I said. "The one who forgot all about the modern technology of a toothbrush and some Crest."

Madison replied, "Ah, yes. Code Yellow. What a bitch. She obviously lacks class if she swooped in to steal your boyfriend and didn't brush her teeth all in one day. So, what are you going to do now? I'd appreciate it if you didn't do the whole 'Eat my weight in sweets' bit or go down the 'Let's do something crazy with my hair!' route. It's not a good road, trust me. Have you seen my hair? Oh! Oh my God! I've got it!"

I had hoped that she would just fill in the blanks herself, but clearly she needed me to ask before telling me. "Okay, what?"

"Well, I figure it's the time of the year again when you read Salinger, so you should take a page out of Holden's life and come to New York. You know I just got that new place in Greenwich with more than enough room since Leslie went to do that study abroad art program in Florence and I also know that you probably haven't reminded your parents that it was time to pony up the cash for your classes. What's stopping you?"

Madison let me sit and ponder this for a moment. Had it really happened that quickly? Had I found a place mere minutes after discovering that someone needed to open the cage door and let me roam free? I obviously couldn't let her think that I hadn't already realized that I needed a change in location. No, she would be sad that she hadn't thought this up first. Instead, I decided to boost her ego a bit.

I said, "You know what, Mad? That sounds exactly like what I need. There's plenty of good music and art all over the city and it would be a total change of pace for me. I'm going to go and call my parents but let's just consider it a done deal, all right? I'll call you to let you know when to come and get me from JFK."

The calls to my parents were easier than I could have imagined. After explaining to them the situation and my feelings on where my life is going, they understood and threw the Benjamins in my account. As long as I was in the continental U.S., they were okay with it. Besides, they couldn't exactly tell me no. As I sat at the computer, I wasn't entirely sure whether New York City was the place for me, or Madison's apartment for that matter. Regardless, I decided I should give it a whirl, seeing as I just gave a nice sum of money to Travelocity to fly my ass out there. That little Roaming Gnome gets me every time.

I called Madison back and all I said when she answered was, "Tuesday, 10:45 in the morning. JFK. I'll be there, will you?"

I could hear the smile in her voice and knew the answer before I heard her say, "Get ready for the city that never sleeps, bitch!"

"Luckily for them, I just happen to be nocturnal."

She laughed and said, "I'll see you Tuesday!"

And I knew that Tuesday would be the start of something completely new and invigorating. I looked around and hoped that when I came back, I would have a new outlook on everything I was staring at. I would be able to appreciate the people in my life, the places I've seen and the things I've learned. If not, well shit, at least I spent some time in the city of new beginnings.

I packed and repacked until I managed to shove half of my clothing into the suitcases I was taking with me. It seemed as if time had flown through the last four days and I was suddenly waking up Tuesday morning. The airport and the flight were a blur. All that mattered was the flashing yellow seat belt sign that told us the descent had begun and we'd be landing any minute. I grabbed my bags and flew to the terminal. I entered the outside arrivals area with my headphones on blaring Frank Sinatra's "New York, New York." I heard a man yelling about a cab not too far away and was already pleased to be in a place so full of life. As numerous cabs came and went, I searched around for the shining purple tresses I knew Madison would be sporting. I spotted them standing next to a cab and ran towards her open arms.

She said, "Alright, let's get these bags back to my place and grab a blanket. It's way too nice of a day to stay inside today."

As we put my luggage in the truck and slid onto the cracked leather seating, I asked, "So, where do you want to go then?"

Madison gave the directions to her apartment to the driver, sat back in the seat and replied, "Well, duh. We're going to Central Park."

CHAPTER TWO

Kiernan

It was like that song from *Once*, the moment I saw her smile radiate across the park and her hair fly in the breeze as she spun around to the music that filled her ears. I wanted to know her, everything there was to know about her. I wanted to know her favorite color, her favorite movie, her favorite season. I didn't care what it was we talked about or when, as long as I was in her presence. You know how sometimes they say in songs that something like an electric current filled their veins when they saw a girl that simply dazzled them? I always thought that was a load of complete trash until now. I had never seen someone look so beautiful and captivating as she was back where I spent my entire life until now.

I guess we should have started there as opposed to me bumbling on about a gorgeous girl across the park. Hi, I'm Kiernan. I'm from a little town that no one cares about. I grew up strait-laced and never stepped out of bounds. Adventure was never on my radar, but after two years of ridicule in college, I figured I'd fly down the rabbit hole and end up in New York. It's not exactly Wonderland, but at least it offered me some sort of freedom to experience new things.

Two years of college, you say? That's simply not long enough to have graduated and be spending time around Strawberry Fields of Central Park at the crest between the heat and the turning of the leaves on collegiate grounds. You're right, though. That isn't long enough. I've decided to take a year off because I realized that I've yet to live. I am younger than everyone due to skipping a grade, but the sentiment remains the same. I figure school will always be there, but youth? Excitement? It's fleeting in most people's lives, and I want to have stories to tell.

Take my friend Adam, for example. He'd traveled to more places before he was 11 than I have in my entire life. At this point in my life, tales of Disney World don't really pull off that "wow" vibe anymore. But this guy, I mean, he could talk to you for hours about a single trip and you felt like you were there right there alongside him as he scaled mountains, wooed countless girls that spoke in different tongues and swam through oceans. You could just about taste the gnocchi in Italy and smell the air in Austria. There went my story about the character breakfast with Mickey and friends. Damn, just when I thought I had one up on this guy.

It's not even that I just wasn't well-traveled globally. Apart from the states bordering my homestead of North Carolina and visiting Florida, I haven't ventured very far beyond that. I've just turned 20 and have yet to see all that the fair country I live in has to offer, let alone the way other cultures go about their lives. That's not to say I wasn't curious what else was out there. I just never suggested anything to my parents and likewise. While kids were heading out to lay on the sands of the Caribbean for spring break, I was getting ready to explore Memphis, Tennessee in all its glory for the second or thirteenth time. I think it's safe to say our yearly Elvis excursion solidified my father as an Elvis fanatic.

No, the adventures to other lands that I took were the ones that spread across my imagination as I read countless books. If I couldn't live a lavish life of adventure, I might as well read about those that did. Since I could remember, I was the kid who had his nose in the spine of a book whenever he could. I read books about valiant knights and social outcasts and quirky friendships. They brought what people would like to call "a sparkle" into my lackluster life. I'm pretty sure that you can gather by now that I'm incredibly shy. (If that wasn't a given by now, then you might want to see your local physician, because you could potentially have a psychological problem regarding your reasoning skills.) Then again, this was to be expected. My parents have been bookworms all of their lives as well. They have taught philosophy and European history at Duke University all of my life. Talking about what book any one of us was reading at that time was not uncommon dinner table talk.

The problem is, after so long, your imagination starts to become a little tired with thinking up its own images. That's when you go to a different medium of entertaining your wildest dreams. This is the point in your life where you become a movie buff. It's not something that you intend on doing, it just sort of happens. You fall in love with leading ladies like Ginger Rogers, Judy Garland, Lauren Bacall and Katherine Hepburn. That is, if you happen to have a healthy relationship with Turner Classic Movies, like I so obviously do.

As I sat on the plane heading towards JFK this morning, these are the aspects of my life that I thought about before picking up the latest Chuck Palahniuk where I'd left off while waiting in the terminal. It's an odd thing to sit back and try to evaluate your life. Every thought that lead up to my leaving ate away at me the whole flight and I had to read some passages over before I even understood what I meant. You wonder why you let certain experiences pass you by or why you allowed people to sometimes walk all over you because they knew you didn't have it in you to turn someone down. My comprehension skills began to wane and I was forced to put my book down. The next thing I knew, the captain was announcing our descent and was hoping we had a wonderful stay in New York City or wherever our connecting flight would lead us.

I felt the woman next to me placing her belongings back in her bag as her gaze seemed to wander onto my profile. I see her smile out of the corner of my eye as she leans towards me and asks, "First time to New York?"

Slightly confused and nervous as to why she asked, I said, "What? Me? Oh, yes. It is."

She continued to smile and asked, "Are you going to school there or are you just visiting? You look far too young to be going there for business."

"Do I? I suppose that's good. Uh, I'm going there to take a break, I suppose." What is wrong with me? I should have left the nerves back at home. Wasn't I trying to break out of my shell? Get it together, man!

The woman lets out a small laugh. It sounds rich and genuine. She says, "You don't sound too sure about that. I'm Molly, by the way. If you intend on staying here for awhile, you might want to get used to meeting new people."

Molly held out her hand with deep red polished nails. I looked at it for a moment before realizing it was rude to not shake her hand.

"Hello, Molly. I'm Kiernan. It's nice to meet you."

Withdrawing her hand, she replied, "Well, aren't we cordial for someone who seems to be pretty shy." For a second, I wonder if she's telepathic and can hear the words in my head falling over one another. We exchange looks before she continues. "So, you're taking a break, huh? How long is this break exactly?"

I contemplate this for a moment. I hadn't really thought about it, to be honest. "It's an undecided time frame at this juncture."

"Well, everyone needs a break every now and again. Of all the places in the world to explore life, why did you choose New York?"

I look down at my hands as the plane hits the tarmac. I also hadn't really thought about the answer to this question either. Frankly, I never thought anyone would ask. As numerous answers flooded my brain instantaneously, I just blurted out as many as I could before my breath gave out. "Well, it embodies what America stands for. New York is a representation of the opportunities and diversity of our country. It's a place that's bright lights and busy streets always offer you something new and exciting to see. You see so many walks of life and really get a feel for what the world has to offer, you know?"

I take a deep breath and hear the sound that indicates that its time to unfasten our seatbelts and begin to gather up our luggage. I look at the woman sitting next to me out of the corner of my eye in case she might think I'm a little loopy. Instead of getting the "Okay, crazy. That was fun" look, I catch her smiling and I flash her a meager grin before unbuckling my seatbelt.

"Do you always get embarrassed whenever you speak? Or is it just when one of those shy people outbursts happen?" she asks. "Trust me, I've seen those before."

People begin to file out of the plane as Molly stands and picks up her bag. It's the first time I get the chance to look at her. Her cropped red hair frames her face just right and pulls the green hues out in her eyes that make me feel like she's genuinely interested in what I have to say. I wonder if the people here are going to be as nice as her. While we wait for the opportunity to exit our row of seats, she looks at me. "Well, it's refreshing to hear a reason for coming here other than girls saying they want a life like Carrie Bradshaw's. Who gets that? No one."

We walk out towards the terminal in silence. Before walking ahead, she turns to me and says, "You should really talk more. It can get you far in this city. And get used to meeting new people, too. It'll happen a lot here. Some might not be the nicest people you've ever met, but you never know. One of those people might change your life." She pauses to check the time on her phone. "It was wonderful meeting you. I hope you find what you're looking for."

Before I can reply with the hopes that I find what I'm looking for as well, she's lost in the sea of people. I start to feel the proximity of busy people waiting to fly to other locations and realize I should really get out of here. I walk to the arrivals area outside and hop in line to get a cab. Thankfully, I didn't have to wait long. As I was waiting for the next cab to pull up, I looked around the area. There were families, businessmen yammering into their cell phones and tourists clad in visors and fanny-packs. Just as the cab pulled up, I noticed a girl not too far away searching around as she listened to her headphones.

"Are you going to get in that cab or what? Some of us have places to be today before the sun goes down!"

The angry man shook me back to reality and made me realize I had been staring at the girl. What was I supposed to do? She was gorgeous. I hastily threw my luggage into the trunk and climbed into the backseat. I told the driver the address of my cousin's Upper East Side apartment and just as we pulled out of the airport area, my phone started ringing in my pocket. It was my cousin Travis and since he was the one allowing me to stay at his place rent free-during my sabbatical, I figured I shouldn't ignore it.

"Hello?"

"Hey, Hobbit boy. Where are you?"

Rolling my eyes, I tell him that I'm walking through an Elfish village in the hopes of finding information on how to destroy some mysterious ring that seems to cause nothing but problems.

"I'm in a cab. What's up?"

I can hear people in the background telling him that he needs to hurry up. "Nice. Okay, listen. This photo shoot is running a little bit longer than I thought, so just ask the doorman to hold your bags until we get back. Do you want to meet me in Central Park? We can start getting those ridiculous tourist traps off your list."

"Yeah, that sounds like a good plan."

"Great. Don't go wandering off either or I won't give you the goods to grow your magic beanstalk."

With that, Travis hangs up the phone and I'm left shaking my head wondering what I was thinking deciding to come and stay here with him. If nothing else, this will be quite an interesting time in my life. While I let myself consider the possibilities, I don't even realize that we're already in front of his apartment building. I pull my luggage out of the trunk and pay the cabbie. Looking up, it's hard to imagine that I would be staying in such an expensive neighborhood. Again, it seems that I forget where I am as the constant stream of horns and shouting brings me back.

I take my bags in and kindly ask the doorman to hold them until I can return with Travis later, seeing as I have yet to obtain a key to the apartment. He politely obliges as I grab a notebook and pen from my bag and he tells me the quickest way to get to Central Park. Walking along the streets, it becomes impossible to take everything in. Within seconds I am overwhelmed by the life reverberating off of every street corner and pane of glass in every window. Every person you pass looks different from everyone else. When you go from small town to big leagues in just a short plane ride, you realize just how much you've been missing.

Just as I start to absorb everything, I see the park stretching out before me. It's impossible for a smile to not spread wide across my face. I cross the street and walk until I find a bench to wait for Travis on. Once I text him where I'm at, I start to look around the park and all that seems to be going on. It amazes me that the majority of the city can be hectic all day but there is this part where everything is wide open and easy going. Wanting to remember every detail, I take out my notebook and begin to write. There are people running down the path that winds through the grassy areas, a Frisbee being passed around not too far away and children coloring. Soon I have pages filled with every detail I can see and margins comprised of ideas for stories that should be told.

"Do you want to seem cool or what? You know intellectuals litter this city with their 'I'm so cool because I read philosophy and write poetry' bullshit, right?"

I look up at the tall figure standing above me. "Honestly, it's always lovely to see you, Travis. You are the picture of family values and kind hospitality."

He shrugs. "Yeah, well. I also got the looks, so it seems that it just sucks to be you, man."

I stand up as the two of us start to walk at a leisurely pace through the park. Sometimes I wonder why I maintain such a close relationship with Travis. For starters, we are different in every aspect. I often wonder how he can get so many women with such a "winning" and "kind" personality, but he gets away with being such a jerk because of the way he looks. Travis is a handsome guy by any human's standards. He's about 6'3" with closely cropped blond hair, pearly whites that didn't even require braces and it was like he came out of the womb with the build of a Spartan. I'm a little on the shorter side (5'8" to be exact) with dark hair and an inability to sound so crass in public. I guess that's why he became a model and made enough money to live on the Upper East Side of Manhattan.

The two of us talk and laugh for a few minutes as we chat before Travis interrupts and asks why exactly I'm here.

"I'm not sure exactly. I guess I just needed to do something for me. You know, see what else was out there since I've never really seen anything."

He nods his head and fishes his cell phone out of his pocket. "I can accept that. I was wondering when you would finally, you know, live. You'll see a whole lot of new things around here. Hey, hold up for a second."

We stop walking as he responds to whatever it is that has him so transfixed on his phone. Travis slides his phone back into his pocket and looks around the park. He smiles and pats me on the shoulder. He cocks his head towards two girls in the grass not too far from where we're standing.

"Like those two girls over there, for instance. Seriously. How many girls run around North Carolina with a full head of purple hair? Exactly. Not that many, right? And the other one she's with just looks like a hardcore bitch."

That's when I saw her and felt like every word in that song was applicable to how I felt in that moment of seeing her. I couldn't understand how Travis could think ill of her when she was smiling like the world was at her fingertips. I couldn't stop staring. I hope she didn't notice because that would be really creepy. Should I go talk to her? No, she looked like she went for guys like Travis instead of me. Then all at once I realized that this was the girl I had glimpsed earlier at the airport. By now, it seemed virtually impossible for me to focus anywhere else but on the sight of her.

"Actually, I saw that girl at the airport earlier. Not the one with the purple hair. That must be her friend. I doubt she's a bad person."

Travis looks at me and raises an eyebrow. "Let's go talk to them and find out."

My eyes snap away from her and back onto my cousin. "What? No. Why would we do that?"

He puts a hand on my shoulder and stares at me for a moment before saying, "Well, not only do I want action, but I can just tell that you need it pretty bad yourself. You broke up with Jenny how long ago? Exactly. I'll take Crayola and since you keep staring at the real-life gossip girl, you can take her. Now come on."

Shaking my head and looking between him and the two girls I tell him that it's fine. I can stay here while he goes and talks to them. He smacks his head and feigns surprise as he looks back at me.

"That's right! I completely forgot that your balls never dropped and you go silent around girls. When are you going to get over that? You've had girlfriends. How? I don't know, but man up, okay?"

Before I comprehend that slap in the face, Travis is already walking towards where the two girls are sitting. I shake my head and trail behind him coming to grips with the fact that I just don't have a say in the matter.

16

CHAPTER THREE

Ava

"Hey, what's up?"

"Oh my God," I said out loud. I looked the other way as fast as I could and stood up. Why do guys seem to flock to females that are either in serious relationships or just coming out of one? It's like a carnal smell. Gross.

"We were just leaving, actually." I'm sorry, did I just hiss that at them? Whoops. Suddenly Madison stands up and looks at me like she was the one personally struck with the hiss venom.

"What? No, we weren't." She looks at me like I'm bonkers, turns back with a smile, extends her hand and introduces herself to what I can already tell is a terrible idea.

He smiles back at her with a toothpaste ad set of teeth and says, "I'm Travis. It's nice to meet you. This is my mute cousin Kiernan."

I don't think I have every seen someone's head fall so low in embarrassment so fast in my life. He's already docking points for being such an ass. I already can't stand this conversation. My arms are crossed to show that I simply don't wish to speak to him and I'm looking the other way, but I hear him ask my name.

Of course, Madison is always willing to lend information out. "This is my friend Ava. She just flew in to stay with me for awhile."

She looks at me like I'm supposed to offer up some sparkling pearl of wisdom to impress this kid, but that's just not going to happen. "Yes, I'm sure that he's very interested in the day we've had so far."

Realizing that this just wasn't a rodeo that that cowboy wanted to enter, he shook his head and looked back at Madison. "Anyway, what are you doing later? Kiernan just got here today, too. He's never been to New York. Why don't you two come along and help show him a part of the city with me tonight?"

Was that a giggle I just heard? Did she just pull out the move where she peers up at him as she tucks a stray piece of hair behind her ear? This girlish tendency won't do. Before she can say that we can work something out to accommodate these fools, I sidle up next to her, place my hand on her arm and ask them to excuse us for a moment. We walk just out of earshot of Tweedle-Dee and Tweedle-Dipshit and I offer up one of my "you've got to be kidding me" looks I've been known for.

Madison crosses her arms and says, "What? It could be fun! Plus, homeboy is slamming!"

We look back to where the two guys are standing and talking. We look the two of them up and down and I see what I'm left with. Conversation will already be dull if I am forced to join in on these shenanigans. That doesn't sound like a great first night here, so I turn back to face her. "Are you kidding me? I just got here and you're already on the prowl for guys!"

The weight of Madison's hands on my shoulders is light but forceful all at once. "Listen, I know you're upset about what happened and would rather stab any guy in the leg than be around them, but I'm not going to quit my life just because you want to. This could be good for you! Now, perk up and put on a smile. We're going out tonight."

Was that a wink? Oh my God, I can already sense her determination with this one. She looks over at them one more time and says, "And with any luck, he'll be putting out later. Do you want to stay here or would you like to frown next to me while I do some work?" She thinks about that for a second and says, "Actually, stay here. You're sending out hate vibes that aren't helping me."

I throw up my hands in defeat as she walks back to the two guys. Instead of focusing on my impending evening of doom being plotted, I look around the park. When that gets boring after three seconds, I look back at them. Do I have an open for business sign flashing in neon across my forehead? This kid and his buddy are trying to chat me and Madison up like it's open season. Well, no. I take that back. Blondie over there was doing all of the talking. He was definitely ripped under his button down and cardigan combo and boot cut jeans. I don't think I caught his name, Triton? Trifecta? Who cares, but his mother should have named him Richard so the nickname "Dick" would be appropriate. This waste of a good dip in the male gene pool was arrogant as hell. He reminded me of someone who deserved a nice junk punch. As per usual, Madison had already seemed to have hit her sweet tooth with this piece of eye candy.

The guy he was with was thin and taller than me, but then again, who isn't taller than my towering 5'2" frame? It's not a gold medal accomplishment, but let's say he was around 5'9". Kiernan was his name and I only remembered it because it had caught me off guard. I hadn't heard a name quite so interesting in awhile. As Dick, as he will henceforth be named, and Smitten Kitten jabbered on, I stole a few glances at Mr. Mystique over there, only to realize that sneak-peeks weren't necessary. Kiernan had his face either glued to the rock he was kicking around or up squinting at the sky. His body language sent him to about a 73 on the uncomfortable scale and I realized that I wasn't the only one less than enthused about the evening's festivities.

King Triton looks over to me and I catch him smiling and waving. The two of them turn and begin to walk away. As I walk back toward Madison, it's hard to not think to myself, "Well, this is going to be an awful night." The Kitten is staring at their backs as they walk the pathway of the park, so I stand there for a second to see if she'll snap out of it. When it's clear that she won't, I tap her on the shoulder. A quick sigh is all I get and all she gets is a swift eye roll.

"Can we bring the focus back to the person standing right next to you? You'll see Mr. High-on-himself later."

"You are so dramatic sometimes, you know that?"

We pick the blanket up off the ground from opposite sides and begin to fold it up. It's the blanket we made out of old concert t-shirts that we didn't want to throw away. It reminds me that we have been through a lot and I resign myself to the idea of hanging out with them. I place it over her arms and ask her what the big plans are for the night.

"We're meeting them at some bar called Mason Dixon down on the Lower East Side. They never really card, so you'll be fine. It's really like the universe is making this easy for me. If the universe had a hand, I'd high-five it right now."

This has got to be a joke. "Well, we better get going then. I'm exhausted and I'm just bursting at the seams to look great later on!" I offer up with false enthusiasm.

Madison's finger is in my face. "Trust me. You will look great tonight. If not, I refuse to be seen out with you." Before I can even let the retort touch my tongue, she continues, "And no, there is no option of looking like you just rolled out of bed tonight because you're not staying in. Let's face it: disputing it with me is entirely futile."

Again, my hands are in the air marking my defeat. Why does that keep happening? Is there some sort of reflex I don't know about, or should I be concerned about the water?

"Fine, fine. I throw up my white flag. But I'm telling you now that this is going to be a bad night. Did you see that kid standing behind him? Kevin or whatever? I know he was kidding but it's like he really was mute."

I feel her arm wrap around my shoulder as we begin to walk our way out of the park. "Sometimes, I really don't know what to say to you."

"I'm just that charming, I'm aware."

After a nice nap and between 13 to 47 clothing changes later (since I was deemed unacceptable), Madison and I are sitting towards the back of a very packed Mason Dixon. Madison bops her head and swerves her shoulders to the beat of the music. We've been here for easily 30 minutes. I know this because I've been checking my phone since we walked in the door. Checking it again and seeing that it's now 32 minutes, I lean across the table and yet again tell Madison that they're late.

Completely unfazed by this, Madison continues to rock her upper body to the music and says, "Who's ever really on time anymore these days unless it's for work or maybe classes? We can wait. It's not a big deal. You certainly have no place to be."

Well, this is going swimmingly. She knows how much I hate waiting, but it seems pointless to bring it up. So, I avert my attention elsewhere to see if there's anyone worthwhile to people watch. Just then I spot Travis scanning the bar looking for the two of us. I resign to pointing this treasure out to Madison who in turn waves her hand in the air towards them and motions for them to sit with us. Don't either of their faces hurt from smiling like morons yet? The Mute seats himself next to me and I can scarcely hear what the other two share between one another. Even though I'm staring at my drink, I can feel the tool's eyes on me. I obviously assume he's about to ask a really mind bending question on metaphysics, but I'm so sadly let down when it's idle chit-chat instead.

"So, you just flew in today, too?" he asks.

Yeah, that's right. You're getting a blank stare right now, buddy.

"I'll take that as a yes. What did you come here for?"

This time I feel like a comment. "To meet suave men like yourself. I was so lucky to have stumbled upon you so early on in my stay." Cue the eye roll, and suddenly playing with the straw in my drink has become the highlight of my night.

"You know, your drinks look a little low. We'll go see what we can do about some fresh ones for you ladies."

He stands and motions for Thing Two to follow him. Once they reach the bar, I can already feel the heat radiating off of Madison.

"Hey, Sassy Suzy. Can we tone down the attitude? It's starting to bug me now and let's not forget where you're staying. He's even offering to buy you a drink, so bring it down a couple of notches, okay?"

"Yeah, fine. I'll see what I can do."

She nods and thanks me for my cooperation which I begrudgingly give up. Travis and Kiernan return to the table each with two drinks in their hands. It's as if he's magnetically drawn to Madison because Travis swivels his body towards her as soon as he sits down. I roughly hear what they say and believe I heard Travis say that he was a model. Well, that explains a lot. They begin to speak softer so neither of us on the other side of the table can hear. I look to my left and see that he's rolling his beer bottle from side to side. I seem to have startled him when I leaned in to thank him for the drink. He hesitates for a moment and says it's no problem.

His hand extends towards me when I introduce myself. I figure I might as well be civil with the kid since we're stuck here. He extends his hand and introduces himself. "It's nice to meet you. I'm Kiernan."

"That's not a name you hear very often."

He hesitates for a moment and decides I won't lodge my straw in his throat, so he turns towards me and says, "I'm not sure I've heard it anywhere before either."

Well, that conversation was short lived. I look down to check my phone so as to avoid awkwardness when I see Kiernan's head again quickly hang low. I glance up to see what caused this and see Madison and Travis in the early first period of tonsil hockey. I lean over to Kiernan and say, "Well, that didn't take long. Let's go."

I nudge him as I grab my phone off the table and sling my bag over my shoulder. When I look over, I see he's staring at me slightly confused. I lean down and ask, "What are you doing? I said let's go. Andale, amigo."

If I'm standing and ready to walk out of this place, why isn't he following my lead? Bug-eyed and shaking my head, he finally takes the hint, stands up and asks what we're doing.

"Oh, I'm sorry. Did you want to stay and watch the show? I didn't think so. We can go walk around or something. It's not like this city has a curfew. Come on."

I catch his arm and pull him towards the exit. I look down both ways and begin to walk with the hopes that he's smart enough to follow.

CHAPTER FOUR

Kiernan

Even though it was the end of August and the temperature during the day was nice, it seemed to have dropped until it was chilly out by the time we were walking at night. Since the two of us left the bar, we managed to walk in silence. Ava hasn't made a break for it, but the silence is still a little unnerving. Sensing that maybe that's how I felt, she finally began to speak.

"So, this is your first time to New York?"

I glance at her to make sure that she isn't asking to ease the discomfort, but because she's interested. When I realized that she might just actually be interested or just a really great actress, I told her that this was indeed my first time here.

"Well, where are you from? If we're going to continue walking around, we might as well get the basics out of the way."

"I'm from North Carolina," I tell her.

"Isn't that where Nicholas Sparks is from? I've read a few of his books. Well, only the ones that got turned into movies, but I like to think that that's beside the point."

Seriously, is that all girls read these days? I'm a literary equal opportunist, but I genuinely don't understand the draw of his work. "Yes, he is."

Why do we keep lapsing into silence? This is somewhat irksome. Before I can get too upset about it or realize that it's pretty much my own doing, she asks a question I don't really know how to answer. "So, why are you here?"

"I'm sorry?" I inquire.

She stops walking and turns towards me. I take that as a clue that I am supposed to stop walking as well and continue to look at the ground.

"I know that you heard me and for the love of God," she said hotly. "There's nothing going on down on the ground. Would you look up?"

I bring my eyes level with hers. They were an interesting shade of green. It was like the water you see in pictures of the Caribbean; light sea foam green that made you want to swim out until you were deep enough to know what lives in the depths. Realizing that she's waiting for me to say something, I shake out of my thought and clear my throat. "I apologize. It's just a habit."

Her eyes look me up and down. It makes me feel like I'm a puppy looking to be adopted in a store window. She looks down the street before looking back at me. "Look, this isn't my ideal night either, but we might as well make the best of it, okay? So, let's try this again. Why are you here in New York? And before you answer, let's lose the man-of-few-words act. It's gross."

Ava tugs on my sleeve to indicate that we should start walking again. This was the third time I had been asked that question in under 24 hours and although my response the first time around seemed adequate, it still wasn't enough. I contemplate how to best answer her and when I come up short, I reply, "I don't know, really. Why did you come here?"

"I don't know. Probably because I wanted to."

Well, that was descriptive. How do I respond to something so riveting? "Oh, okay." And we're back into silence for a minute or two before I formulate just what to say. When I told the woman on the plane earlier about why I'd chosen New York, it seemed so much easier to answer because a destination is never as hard to justify as a reason for leaving is.

"Well, I guess the reason I came here is because I've never really done anything on a whim or outside of my comfort zone, let alone anything for myself really."

Nodding she said, "Mmm. Okay, I like where this is going. Keep it up, kid. We might just get an answer out of you yet."

There's too much and not enough going on in my head all at once. I want this to sound right and dare I say eloquent, but I also don't want her to look at me like I should be picked up by the nice men in white coats. I've just met this girl, yet I'm dying to impress her. I want to know who she is beneath the sarcastic facade and I want her to know everything that has ever happened to me over my brief stint here so far on Earth. This feeling is altogether strange and welcome.

"Well, I mean, after so much ridicule for staying inside the lines, you just want to fly down the rabbit hole. I wouldn't go so far as to say that we're in Wonderland, but this is the perfect stop before getting there."

"Wait, New York City is just a stop?" She laughs. "How do you get to this fabled Wonderland? I'll admit that I'm intrigued and now biting the bait. Let's hear it."

"I see Wonderland as more of a state of mind as opposed to a tangible place." I do? I didn't know that. Let's hope she decides to move on so I don't have to explain myself.

"Oh, yeah? How do you figure?" Why did she need to ask?

Again we lapse into what is now a comfortable silence rather than an awkward one. Ava allows me to gather my thoughts as she looks up at buildings and along the streets at the other people enjoying the night out. I clear my throat to bring her back to what we're talking about.

"Everyone is always striving for this inner happiness where they know and love exactly who they are as a person. Wonderland is exactly that. Sure, the landscape is different for everyone, but that's what makes each of us unique. It's a place you dream up where everything you've ever wanted is within your reach and nothing could ever stop you." Wow, I'm really on a roll here. "The problem is, I have no idea who I really am. That's why I came here. I came to experience everything I had always stayed away from and to take chances. If you don't take chances, you'll never understand who you are or what the world has to offer because you're stuck behind panes of foggy glass."

Suddenly the ground seems interesting again as I catch my breath. I push my hands in the pockets of my tan jacket and hope that this girl, who seems to be wasting her time and stores of energy walking around with me, will just change the subject. Her hand touches my arm. Even through my jacket, I can feel it send waves of heat up through my neck.

25

"Are you okay? You were on a roll there! It was like seeing a light bulb burn too bright and then go out."

"No, I'm fine," I tell her as I casually pull my arm out from under her hand. "I just realized that that was why I really came here. I thought it was just to get away and see things that I'd never seen before, but that's not even close to the truth. I really do have no idea who I am."

This time, instead of merely touching my forearm, she smiles and loops her right arm through my left and tells me, "You know what? There's only a small percentage of people our age who even have a clue as to who they really are. We're all lost in that space between who we were and who we're supposed to be. There's not a single guide book or example out there for us to follow. Don't beat yourself up over that epiphany."

"Thank you. We've been walking a while. Do you want me to walk you back to where you're staying?"

I don't understand why she started to laugh. I was just being nice and don't think a girl should have to walk anywhere alone this late at night. I'll make sure to tell my parents that it gets me laughed at and they should have skipped it when raising me. Damn my growing up in the South.

"Walk me back to where I'm staying? I don't think anyone has ever offered to do that. It's kind of cute. But um, no. That's okay. If you want to go back to your place, that's fine, but Madison's apartment is actually only a couple of blocks away from that bar, so that's bound to be the place those two end up at."

There's a good chance she says what she does knowing that I won't have a proper response for 80% of it. I offer to go back to our apartment so that she can wait it out with some company. Once she agreed, she asks if it's okay if the two of us walk. Why not? It's not as if I've seen the city let alone with someone as glaringly attractive as Ava is. I might as well take advantage of it. The walking together also gives me time to take advantage to really look at her. When she gets rid of what I thought was a permanent scowl, she's really quite radiant.

We walked for quite a long time, but it was made to feel shorter based on the fluidity of our conversation. It was mostly her asking random questions and spewing the most ridiculous and useless facts known to man, but it was still nice. After all that walking, we finally got back to where I was staying with Travis. I unlock the door and as I walk in, I search for the light switch. I can hear Ava already walking in and feel her next to me as she finds the switch before I can. She smirks back at me over her shoulder as she walks towards the chocolate suede couch. The sound of her shoes hitting the floor one by one echoes through the room before she leans back on the couch.

"Well, that's the last time I suggest enjoying the city's scenery over taking a cab. Thank God I'm stubborn."

I have no choice but to go and sit on the couch with her. To not do so might seem rude and that was far from how I wanted her to see me. As I sit down, she picks up her bag and begins rifling through it. She asks, "Where is it?" and before I can ask what it was she was looking for, she pulls her iPod out of the black hole that I have come to learn as a female's purse. Detaching the headphones, she stands up and looks around the room. Again, before I can ask what it is she is looking for, she walks towards the iPod dock sitting on an end table. I watch as she searches for a song in her library and smiles while she hits play. Ava seems to float back to her spot on the couch. The music plays softly and without looking at anything in particular, I can feel her eyes stapled to me.

"This is a great song." Oh, real smooth. That was a terrific way to ease the tension.

"Yeah, it is."

Instead of talking, we allow the music to fill the room. We sit and listen to a few songs. Her music taste was eclectic, though I can't say I knew some of the songs that were played. I was enjoying a song I remember being in *Garden State* when she rather abruptly shook me out of my reverie as she twisted her body towards mine and threw me a look of sheer curiosity. Naturally, this gave me a weird chill down my spine. I knew something was coming that I would find difficult to answer.

"So, what are your views on one-night stands?" she asked.

My face had turned an exquisite shade of scarlet. There was no mirrored surface needed to tell me that. I could feel the warmth flooding my ears. I was spot on with my suspicions. It was a question that I had never been asked. She's getting really good at finding those. There must be a book on questions to ask awkward nerds that I missed. This was about to be quite an awkward conversation, at least on my part. "Excuse me?" I replied.

"I'm pretty sure you heard me. I don't understand why you keep playing like you have a hearing problem. What is your opinion on sleeping with someone you just met and probably won't ever see again? And just so we're clear, the man-of-few-words idea is still outlawed."

I acted as naive as possible, though to be perfectly honest, I hadn't experienced such a thing simply based on the fact that I am awful with girls apart from the two I had dated, and they were the ones to initiate the relationship. Sure, we slept together, but that's because we were dating. I never went out on a Friday night in the hopes of waking up next to Saturday morning's mistake. That just wasn't something that I did.

"I'm afraid I'm not following you." Great, now I look like a lost four-year-old instead of someone who just really wanted to change the subject.

Contemplation filled her face. I'm sure her thoughts were something along the lines of my complete lack of knowledge as to where she was going with this.

"It's usually something that follows a night of, more likely than not, a great deal of Jager bombs and a slight loss of memory until you wake up the next morning with your arm around Jabba the Hut. Although, sometimes you do get Han Solo and you're thankful for that Jager."

The look on my face had to have screamed ALERT: AWKWARD AND UNCOMFORTABLE because she laughed at me again and said, "Or it could be when two people realize their attraction is so great and give it a 'what the hell?' outlook and have at it. I prefer the latter, if we're being honest with each other."

I just sat there looking at her dumbfounded. How could she be that blunt about something so personal? I'm not usually involved in conversations like this. Don't get me wrong, I know exactly what that is, I just don't like talking about it. Apparently, that didn't translate to her so I shook my head to clear the muffled thoughts and finally said something.

"No, I know what they are. I've just never hiked in the Forest of Forgotten Nights. I'm more into the being committed and dating for a little bit before I get into that business," I replied as I threw my head down to look at something on the floor.

"Aww, now aren't you just so cute? Getting a girl a drink, offering to walk her home and now you tell me you wait until you're in a committed relationship before doing the horizontal slide. I think you're on the endangered species list."

I couldn't tell if the smile she gave me after that was a shot at my self-esteem or she was being genuine. I'll just going to stick with thinking that it was genuine because she looked at me to see if I had understood it to be a compliment. When I smiled back, she brightened up and was about to continue when I said, "I don't know. I just feel like you should really know the person before sharing something so intimate."

Again, she smiled but fired off with another question. "Oh, come on. Like you've never seen someone, a celebrity or what have you, and thought about what it would be like to spend a night messing up the sheets with them?

"Oh, well, of course there is an asterisk down at the bottom that states, 'The aforementioned statement whole-heartedly does not apply to the following if the opportunity should present itself.'"

Her hand lightly taps my thigh and a shock runs up my spine. "Well then! A little bit of mischief and a little bit of humor comes peeking out of that shell. Let's hear it then. Who would be on that list?"

"Well, I guess I would say Natalie Portman or Zooey Deschanel. They seem like really nice women."

Yet again, she laughed at me. Was I really that entertaining? This was becoming absurd. "Oh, what's so funny? Just because I said they were nice? Pft. Who would make the cut on your list?"

Somehow, this got her really energized because she shifted her position from lounging back on the sofa to sitting Indian style facing me with her hands up and a smile that announced the crazy train had just pulled into Grand Central Station. She threw her locks of tousled caramel hair over her shoulders and said, "Are you kidding? This could potentially be one of the easiest questions you could ask me. Before I get started, I would like to note that I absolutely love the song that just came on. Anyway, moving on. First, I would start off with Shia LaBeouf or James Franco. Obviously I want to get with the teen scene's wet dreams and see if they deserve said titles. Next would be Justin Timberlake because any girl in their right mind would be stupid to pass up that opportunity. Then there's James McAvoy who is not only gorgeous, but is also Scottish, so I could hit up the international quota."

Is this girl for real? This is a more than one- or two-person list! Who has the time to think about all of this? Wait, I thought she was done. Apparently that was just a pause for breath because she had more to share.

"Oh, and Jack White because he's not only a musician but borderline amazing. Also Joseph-Gordon Levitt because well, he can rock the shoulder-length hair and the buzz cut and always look slamming. Who am I forgetting? Oh! Right! And I would totally go easy for Ron Weasley because he's a ginger and apparently that gene is dying out soon, so with all of that, I'd be hitting points all across the board."

Now, I was the one that was laughing. The look she shot me was something along the lines of confusion and bordered the offended line. For some reason, that made me laugh even more. Ava's irritation was slowly rising and she slammed a very heavy pillow into my side.

"I'm sorry," I managed to get out in between laughs. "You seem to have given this a fair bit of thought and that amused me. I've never met someone with such a list. Please, don't be offended by my laughter."

I could tell that her irritation was slowly fading as a smile crept up through her lips and a laugh surfaced from her mouth. "Oh, you've met them. They just haven't announced and owned it like I have. Now listen to this song. It's great."

Ava puts the pillow back where it was and as she leans back, she closes her eyes. I find it odd that I seemingly can't stop looking at her out of the corner of my eye. I just met this girl today and frankly, until about an hour ago, I didn't even want to be in her presence. In an effort to avert my attention, I ask her what song we're listening to.

"'Plane' by Jason Mraz. It's one of my favorites. This is my favorite part, too."

My eyes are absolutely transfixed on the way her lips form the words, "taste these teeth please and undress me from these sweaters better hurry" as she toys with the necklace that hung on her collar bones. Suddenly all I wanted was those fingers tracing my skin instead. Where did that come from? Heavy breathing ensued and hesitation had a fleeting appearance in my mind. Her eyes fluttered open and my eyes were back staring dead ahead as I interlock my fingers in my lap. I could feel her sitting up and moving closer towards me. She placed her hand on my chin and pushed until I was looking at her straight in the eye. She looked at me with what I have gathered to be hungry eyes. It almost felt like I was the Hershey bar drizzled with almonds that she's been wanting through all of the 40 days and 40 nights of Lent that she swore off chocolate. That look pierced right through me and shocked me straight down to my feet.

Her hand rakes through my hair and she places a soft kiss on my cheek. A brief stop to gauge my reaction and she continues to kiss my cheek once, twice and moves to kiss my jaw line followed by my neck. I feel her lips leave my skin and her hand again applying pressure to spin my face towards hers. I wonder if she can feel the flush of my skin beneath her lips and hands. She analyzes all the aspects of my face before saying, "You know, you sort of look like James McAvoy."

She slowly trails a finger down the length of my arm and her soft hand curves back up over my chest. Seeming to find a natural place on my cheek, her hand pulls my lips to hers. That was too small of a kiss. The tingle she left is begging to spread through the rest of my body. The next thing I knew, we were looking at each other with such intensity. I lean in for a few small kisses and twist my body towards hers. I can't take this anymore. I pull back once more and say "What the hell."

Our kissing became deeper as she intertwined her arms around my neck and I leaned her back down until my body was above hers. Ava's hands wander across my back and under the fabric of my shirt. They feel soft and cool against my skin. I pull back to relieve my shirt of its duties as she does the same with her skirt. I didn't care whether or not this was a one-night stand. All I knew was that if she wasn't mine within the space of time where she placed her hand on my face and the time where my mouth touched hers, I was going to spontaneously combust.

CHAPTER FIVE

Ava

When I woke up the next morning with the sun streaming light through my eyelids, I remembered I was not alone. You know, because the torso my arm was slung across and the warmth of someone else's body heat next to me didn't give that away or anything. I turn my face in the direction of the guy lying next to me.

"Shit," I barely whisper.

I shut my eyes before shifting my attention and looking around the room. Again I look back to him and find myself smiling. He looks so adorable when he sleeps. No. Stop. I can't think like that. This was supposed to be fun and then forgotten. I have to get out of here, but how? Slowly and very carefully, I pull my arm away and quietly slide out of the bed. Thankfully, I put my shirt and underwear back on before going to sleep last night. I search for my skirt that has seemed to take a vacation and forgotten to tell me where it was going. It appears to have also taken my bag on this trip because I can't seem to find either one. Finally, I spot both taking refuge under a chair and slip my skirt on. This escape is going flawlessly, I think. Then I pick up my bag and my cell phone loudly clatters on the floor.

"Fantastic," I say.

Oh, great. Of course that noise woke him up. He's still in the "what was that noise?" phase of waking up, so I'm running out of the room to slip my shoes on and head out the door. Right as I go to turn the knob, I remember my iPod is still on the dock. I race across the room, pluck it from its spot and head back towards the door in the hopes that I can make it out before he catches up with me.

"Where are you going?"

Plan: foiled. Mission: failed. I guess it's back to the drawing boards to figure out better escape plans for next time. What do I do? Should I respond or just really knock the wind out of his sails and walk out? I stand rooted on the spot and decide that it's better to just wait to hear what he comes up with next. I can hear him take two steps in my direction.

"Are you leaving?"

He's relentless this one. I spin to look at him. "Can we not make a big scene about this?"

Well, I haven't seen someone looked that perplexed because of something I've done or said in awhile. "Well, no. I wasn't planning on it. I was just seeing if you wanted to do something later."

"Yeah, about that. No."

I turn once again to take my leave and I hear him ask "Why not?"

Be a big girl, Ava. Look him in the eye when you talk to him about this. I turn and explain to him, "I thought I made it pretty clear last night that this was a one-night-only showing." While still looking baffled, he picks up his shirt off the floor, pulls it over his head and down over what I found out was actually a fit midsection. My hands were not mad at roaming around the contours of his....Anyway, that's not the point.

"But what if I want to see you again?" Another step closer towards me, and another step for me towards the door.

"Well, that's just too damn bad. This was me wanting to feel wanted again after my boyfriend dumped me. You helped me achieve that goal. And you were pretty great for someone who barely speaks until you get the ball rolling. Anyway, there's no strings here. It was fun." Please let me leave when I turn towards the door this time.

"So, it really doesn't matter how I feel?"

The tone of his voice made it impossible to move. He sounded hurt and offended and about 10 other emotions that were currently in use because of me. I can't lose face like this. I turn back to him and shrug. "No, not really. This was all about having a nice hit it and forget it thing. Why would I take your feelings into account?"

"Are you nice just to get what you want?" Another few steps towards me and I'm almost out of room to back into. Kiernan's face contorts with hurt and anger. "Listen, I might not be the most outgoing guy, but I would never manipulate someone into thinking I was generally interested in what they had to say or who they were in order to get what I want."

"Well, I clearly made a mistake in choosing you to take a walk on the wild side with. Oh well. You live and you learn. Can I go now?"

The hurt and anger has now turned to shock and disbelief. I am really tearing this guy up. I'm at the point where I no longer have any idea why I'm being so unintentionally cruel. I mean, what did the kid really do to me? He was nice and intelligent and I'm just being a bitch to cover up my own discomfort with the situation. I usually tended to do that, but this was just bordering the offensive line.

"How can you just talk to people the way you do? Do you have any respect for people, including yourself?"

Before I can feel the sting of what he said, he closes the distance between us and passes me to reach the door.

"I'm the one who made the mistake in thinking that you were someone who I wanted to get to know or who could help me figure out what this world was all about. Thank you for proving me wrong in advance. Now, I will ask you to please leave."

He turns the knob and rips the door open. I feel the blank confusion cloud my face as I look at him before walking out the door. When I turn to say something, to apologize or...I don't even know what I wanted to do, the door slams in my face. I wait for a second, consider knocking but instead walk towards the elevator. I press the button and lean against the wall while I wait. To no one but myself, I say, "Good job, self. You've made another person dislike you. Awesome. Cookie reward later."

I hear the ding of the elevator and head down to the lobby. The late summer sunlight doesn't seem so great anymore and I walk to the subway to head back towards Madison's apartment. The entire time I can't stop thinking about what had just happened. I didn't even realize that my subway card was pushed in the wrong way until I slammed into the bar and heard the automated "Please swipe again." As I sat on the train, I realized that yes, I did in fact need to swipe again. I need to do things right to get to where I need to be in life. When I exited the train, I was so excited about my revelation that I almost forgot about my awful morning.

Unfortunately, when I walked into the apartment and saw Madison sitting at the table on her laptop, everything came flooding back. It's best just to get this out of the way, so I plopped myself down on the chair across from her. I throw in a good morning to lift my spirits but it seems she didn't need a lift in spirits. Without looking up, Madison smiles and says, "Yes, yes, it is a good morning. Good morning indeed."

"I take it you had a good time last night?" I tease, already in full awareness that she had a good time. I stand up and walk to the kitchen to find something to eat.

"A good time last night and a good time this morning. How was your night?"

I could have groaned but I thought against it. Instead, I open a few cabinets and find some crackers to go with the cheese cubes I know are in the refrigerator. "I think it be best if we not mention it."

"Why not?"

I can hear her fingers clack-clack-clacking across the keyboard, so I wonder if she's even paying attention. I grab the cheese from the fridge and sit back down across from her almost entirely deflated. "Because it was all fine and dandy until he decided he wanted to be friends and hang out and do stuff together."

"So, what's wrong with that?"

"Why would I want to be friends with him? We had some fun and that was that. No need to continue speaking."

Madison gives me a reproachful look from behind the screen. "I don't understand why you're being so defensive, but do whatever you want to do. No one's going to stop you. We've learned not to."

Well, that was an early morning ego beat down. How do you come back from that or what had already taken place? Answer: you don't. Therefore, my gaze met the table as Madison continued to punch the keys, which happened to be the only noise in the room. Another few moments and I had to ask the question that was searing patterns in my brain. "Am I really that big of a bitch?"

"What?"

"Am I really that big of a bitch? I mean, do you think I am? The way he treated me this morning was like fifteen slaps in the face. His face was just hurt and offended and sad and oh my God, it was so painful to see that I was the cause of that. And the worst part was, I didn't even know why I was so rude to him. I wanted so badly to be away from that feeling of using him that it just came flowing out."

Finally, she stops stabbing the keys and looks up at me for the first time since I walked in. "Do you really want the truth?"

"Yes," I say and lean forward. "I really want the truth."

"Yes, I do. I'm used to it, but it's just getting worse. It's like you're turning into a cynic and want everyone else to get on that train with you. You can't keep treating people like puppets in the Ava Sinclair show. It's not always about you. Sometimes? Sure, but not all the time."

This is a real blast. "It's not like I do it on purpose. He made me feel like a bad person, like I should fix it or deal with the fact that I will one day become a reclusive cat lady."

Madison looks close to shocked and surprised. "Are you having a breakthrough? If you are, I might need to go back that boy some cupcakes or something to thank him."

Again, you can't come back from these kinds of statements, so I continued to look at my hands lying on the table. I can't even bring myself to look at my best friend when I ask, "Am I really that bad of a person? I didn't think that I was."

She sighs and closes her laptop. Coming around to my side of the table, she takes my hand in her own and says, "No, you're not a bad person. You're a good person when you want to be. You do have an attitude and a sudden negative outlook on the world but no one's perfect. You can always fix what you don't like. That's the beauty of society."

I pull my hand free. "I feel like I should apologize or something. I really should not have been so unnecessarily rude to him. He was really sweet."

Madison reaches across the table and picks up her laptop. She walks towards her room and stops at the door. "Just do whatever you have to do. If you want to apologize, go over there and do so. I know you better than that and once you get something in your head, you have to do it. I'm going to sleep. I didn't get much last night."

Why did she just wink at me again? We need to knock that out of her system. It's getting creepy. She shuts the door and leaves me alone with my thoughts. I lean back and once again say to no one else but myself, "I really am a bitch. Fuck."

Three days later, I weasel my way up to the door that was recently slammed in my face. I've spent the last three days going over how I treated him and realizing that that's not the type of person that anyone wanted to know. Plus, he wasn't the type of person who deserved to be treated as such just because I was acting stupid. I consider not knocking and just walking away. I go over what I planned on saying and attempt the knock again. When I realize I'm acting childish, I rap my knuckles against the door.

When Kiernan opens the door, I feel like the bully that stole his lunch money. I have nothing else to say other than "Hi" and offer him a weak smile as an olive branch. Apparently he's pretty well stocked on those and doesn't want mine because he continues to look stone-faced and asks, "May I help you?"

Down go my eyes to the ground. I notice how when Kiernan looks at the ground, it's because he's afraid. Unfortunately, when I look at the ground, it's due to shame or embarrassment. He's already winning here.

"Yeah, I guess I deserve that. Okay, Listen. I'm not very good at this because honestly, I rarely do it, but I know I treated you poorly the other day. Well, poorly is an understatement, but I was unnecessarily rude and you didn't deserve that."

"Is this supposed to be an apology?"

My eyes snap up to look into his. "I said I wasn't good at this, okay? I'm sorry. I know I'm a bitch but there's always room for change, right?"

And we're back to the awkward silence. My eyes get called back into an emergency meeting with the ground. When he still doesn't say anything, I figure it best just to say what's on my mind. "I really am sorry. I really was interested in what you had to say. I know I shouldn't even be asking this, but do you want to spend the day together?" I glance up at him to see if his face gives way to any emotion. When he looks confused, I continue, "We can see a bit of the city and get to know each other. I feel bad for the way that I treated you. There has to be something that I can do to make it up to you."

It goes silent for a few moments and then he places those brilliant blue topaz eyes on me as he steps back, giving me room to enter the apartment. "Come on in. There's no need for you to be standing out there."

A faint smile creases my face and I walk in, but stop in the doorway once he shuts the door. The wave of relief that washes over me feels refreshing, but I know that I'm still not at the shores of forgiveness. I keep that in mind as I watch him cross the room in just a few strides and put his phone in his left front pocket. He places a bookmark between the pages he left off on and puts the book on a small coffee table. He turns back to where I'm standing and asks, "So, what would you like to do?"

"You know, I don't know." I'm trying to tread as lightly as I can here. "Anywhere where we can talk is fine by me. Or outside. It's a really nice day out."

He walks back to me and flashes a smile. "I'm sure that we can figure something out."

Placing his hand on the small of my back, he leads me towards the door and out into the hallway.

CHAPTER SIX

Kiernan

"There's something about this place," I thought to myself as we meandered through Times Square and gawked at the never-ending hustle and bustle of the entire city as it turned from nightlife to morning light. You can go to Vegas, Chicago, Miami or LA and probably never experience what you do in the Big Apple (or so I've heard). Here is the place among the bright lights and the hidden spots that you can truly escape the mess of real life. New York City is a world and a lifestyle all its own. I had completely gotten lost in my own thoughts that I had forgotten I was with Ava until she intervened.

"Thanks for today. It was a lot of fun."

I couldn't help but smile. "It was. I'm sorry you had to do tourist things."

She waved her hand in the air. "No, don't even worry about it. You've never been here. I haven't even done the tourist things and I've been here plenty of times. Like I said, it was fun. We did manage to hardly learn anything about each other, though. I thought that that was the main goal. Or did I imagine that?"

We stopped at a corner to cross to the section that splits Broadway in half.

"Yeah, I guess you're right. It was a little hard to do that between mouthfuls of New York pizza and telling elementary school field trip war stories." We both laugh. "Why don't we give it a try now. So, why did you come here? You never really told me."

She hesitates before answering. "It's like I said. Because I wanted to."

We cross the street and stand at what feels like the center of everything. Cars are whooshing past us on either side, there's so much noise, and the lights never seem to turn off. Why is this such a difficult question for her to answer? It seems like she's hiding something. Actually, it seems like every time a really personal question came up, she sealed the cat flap that lead into her room of brick walls. It's so strange. I'm sort of over that idea, so I try again. "Well, right, but that doesn't tell me anything. How about giving me the real reason behind your expedition to discover this brave new world?"

Staring up at the neon lights of the MTV studios, she says, "I just got tired of my life, that's all." Ava turns and starts to walk away. Where is she going? She yells at me for giving up so little yet she's allowed to stop the conversation whenever you breach her comfort zone. That doesn't seem very fair. I catch up to her, grab her arm and spin her towards me.

"Why do you keep doing that?"

"Doing what?" she muses.

I let go of the loose grip on her arm. "You keep avoiding giving a real answer to any question. In the two days that I have known you, your responses are either snarky and borderline rude or devoid of anything substantial roughly 67% of the time."

We stand looking at each other. Her face is a look of mingled curiosity and mine is somewhat shocked at the harshness of my words. This sudden burst of confidence is liberating, but bizarre.

"I'm sorry. That was rude."

She tugs on my sleeve and stands at the crosswalk. I don't want to say anything else in the hopes that she'll answer. We cross the second section of Broadway and continue walking. It's almost two blocks before she decides to help me around one of her mental road blocks.

"I wouldn't say that what you said was rude. It's easier to be a bitch than it is to be Miss Sugar and Spice. I don't answer with anything substantial because I sort of don't trust anyone. Yes, I'm sure that that is a shocking plot twist in my life story, right?" She looks ahead and shakes her head like she caught herself doing something wrong. "That and if I tell someone what I'm feeling, this whole black-soul-type facade would just crumble away," she adds hastily.

Seriously. We make progress and the use of humor as a defense mechanism makes an appearance. I ask, "Does that matter to you?"

"What? What people think of me?"

I simply nod my head to urge her to continue.

"Sometimes. But that's not why I'm here. Actually, if you're looking for me to be honest with you, which I know that you do, I felt this way before what Madison assumes brought me here, which is that I broke up with my boyfriend and I take break-ups pretty seriously." She pauses. "I honestly have no fucking clue why I'm telling you any of this, but having unlimited time to just...think has really slapped me in the face."

Ava draws a deep breath before continuing. "Even before all of that happened with D-bag 3000, I was in this really weird place. I couldn't figure out what it was, but it definitely took breaking up with him to bring it to a head, so to speak. The fact that I'm in college already is incredibly terrifying. I mean, it's not as if I'm ancient or anything, but it seems like just yesterday I was shopping at the Children's Place and now all of a sudden I'm wondering what my next overpriced pair of shoes is going to be. It's like the years between naivety and real life just flew by."

She stops speaking and continues to walk on. Although I don't want to push my luck, obviously I have to press on if I'm going to get to know this girl that was turning out to be more like a maze than a human.

"Well, that seems like it was quite a slap in the face," I said.

"Yeah, I guess you could say that. I suppose this was the cold splash of water to ease the sting of that solid backhand life threw at me."

Instead of stopping her words, she stops walking and glances up at a beautifully structured building. I stop and place a small distance between us so she can gather the thoughts that seem to be spinning an intricate web in her head. The noise of the city seemed to dissipate in those moments of silence.

Finally, she began to speak again. "I just want to find that kaleidoscopic vibrancy of life that has taken a backseat to all the monotony of the latter half of my adolescence. I was hoping that maybe I could find it here, but now I'm not even sure if that's possible."

I close the space between us and place my arm around her shoulder for a means of comfort. "I know that this might seem hard to hear right now, but not everyone can pull off the Peter Pan mentality. The rest of us just need to grow up and remember that the most important thing we can take from our childhood is the realm of possibility. As long as we're as optimistic as we were when we were younger, life will be okay."

Somehow being around her made it easy for me to sledgehammer down the brick walls that I had built around *myself*. I'm surprising myself with each statement like that, flying out of my mouth like a circus performer shooting out of a canon. I just reminded myself of some Walt Disney quotes about the blurred lines of childhood and adulthood, but I don't think I should ruin my wise sentiments just now. Ava seems equally impressed by what seems to flow effortlessly from my brain to my lips and through her auditory system because she smiles up at me and slings an arm around my waist.

"Yeah, I guess you're right. I suppose I was just so caught up in life speeding towards me that I really was chasing Peter Pan like a Lost Boy. Great analogy. I'll remember that one."

God, her eyes could swallow me whole. I almost wish she would stop looking me in the eye because her eyes alone seem to halt my speech. When I tried to thank her, I just make a noise and look ahead. Instead of having to become embarrassed by a conversational blunder that could spoil the mood, Ava saved it and started walking again.

"It's getting really late. I think it's time to head home and go to bed. We barely made a dent in this city today. If we're going to continue on seeing all the tourist traps of this place, I have to get some sleep," she protested.

"You want to do this tomorrow?" I wondered. It seems I was unable to mask the surprise sprinkled with excitement in my voice. Great. I sound like a ten-year-old with a brand new bicycle on Christmas.

"Well, yeah. Why wouldn't I? Didn't we just establish that this was fun?" she asks as she removes her arm and walks to the curb, flinging her hand in the air to hail a cab. I stay standing where I am as a cab pulls up seconds later. She looks back towards me and tells me to give her a call tomorrow. Before I can even respond, she jumps into the car and it speeds off down the street. I guess I have plans for tomorrow and hopefully the rest of my stay.

For the last five days, the two of us spend hours trolling the various neighborhoods of Manhattan. We've endlessly talked but yet I still feel as if I don't know who she really is. I ponder this as I walk towards the building where Ava temporarily lives with Madison. I ring the buzzer and wait for a response.

"Who is it?" I can hear the knowledge of it being me in her voice.

"Were you expecting someone else?" I ask. I hear the lock click on the door and I make my way up the three floors to their door. She opens the door with a smile and invites me in. Does she not know what time it is? Did she forget that we had plans? I walk in confused by her clothing choice and close the door behind me.

"Hey, are you- you're not wearing that out, are you?"

She looks down at her pajamas and laughs. "Yeah, about that. Do you think we could halt this whole Lois and Clark thing? Just for today. We've been making this city our bitch for almost the entirety of the last week. I think my legs are about to stage a mutiny. Besides, what have we really learned about each other except the surface bits that anyone can know?"

Whoa, how did we get on the same wavelength? Is she actually going to tell me more about herself? I'd been waiting and hoping that she would offer something up, but it never happened. "I guess you're right. So, what should we do?"

Ava walks towards a bedroom and stops in the doorway. "First, you're going to stop awkwardly standing by the door. It makes me feel like you're already plotting your escape. Second, are you going to follow me in here or not?" She turns to walk in, but thinks the better of it and looks at me. "Oh, and by the way, I'm not looking for any bedroom frolicking."

Why am I still standing here? Ava just disappeared into her room. I should probably follow her in there. When I walk in, I see her sitting down in the middle of her bed as she scans her iPod. I stop in the doorway because I'm an idiot. She invited me in here! There's no reason for me to be hesitating like this. Ava looks up at me, perplexed.

"The bed is not going to bite you. Sit down already."

After removing my shoes, I sit down on the edge of the bed. I don't understand why I am so uncomfortable right now. Just over a week ago I was having some big kid playtime with her and now I can't even sit on a bed with her. How old am I again? Making it worse, Ava places the iPod on the player and sprawls across the length of the bed.

"You are hopeless. Lay down. Close your eyes. Enjoy the damn music."

I realign myself on the bed and lay down next to her. She smiles and closes her eyes indicating I should do the same. We laid there and allowed the music to fill up the silence between us. It was one of those silences that doesn't feel uncomfortable and doesn't require either party to speak. I like the feeling that stirs up. We lay like that for a song and when the next one starts, I open my eyes to see her still smiling and moving her head to the music. Another ten seconds and she says, "I can feel you looking at me, you know."

She opens her eyes and sees the blush warming my face. I probably look like a clown. I open my mouth to say something, but she beats me to it. "And before you ask, yes, music is a big deal to me. And no, I'm not psychic. I just know that's what you're thinking."

Lifting an eyebrow, I say, "Oh really?"

Her gaze floats back to the ceiling and she nods. "Oh yeah. And next, I bet you're going to ask me why it is that music means so much to me."

"Do I even really need to speak, Miss Cleo?"

"No not really. You're just decoration at this point."

I can sense a silence coming on and now that she's finally talking about herself, I can't allow that to happen. I have to get her to keep talking.

"Oh, well. Don't try to avoid the question. Why does it mean so much to you? I think that's a pretty good starting point for our foray into each other's personal business. The idle chit-chat has overstayed its welcome, don't you think?"

Her eyes flutter shut once more and she takes a deep breath. I can smell that sweet scent of success as she resigns herself to divulging something important.

"Fine. It's that feeling of sitting around with nothing to occupy you but the music filling up the room or your headphones. It's the immense rush of the lights going down right before a band walks out onto the stage, ready to play the songs that wreak havoc on your emotions and, to quote Fall Out Boy, 'make your heart swell and burst.' Even that doesn't compare to standing in the back of a crowded room and the crescendo of screams and the roller coaster arms flying in the air start to swallow the room up as you feel the floor start to shake with feet jumping up and down to the words and music that fills the soundtrack to your own life. Not to mention that there's an artist, album or song to go with virtually any mood."

She looks at me very seriously and asks, "Does that answer your question?"

I paused before responding, due to the fact that I had no words that could form a proper response. Hearing about something I just listen to because it sounds good and not for any real reason in a new light was like finding a crumpled twenty dollar bill in your jacket; it was exciting. There are albums, artists and songs that I'm attached to, but that way she just described her feelings makes me want to really listen to them, to feel what the artist wants you to feel. It was incredible to hear the detail and conviction with which she talked about music.

"Sorry," she said. "I tend to come on a bit strong when I talk about something like this. We should just move on to putting you on the spot. What pulls at your heart strings?"

Well, now I'm perplexed. Here she was going on and on about how much music means to her and then she pulls a U-turn to take us back to where we started. I really need to invest in a roadmap if talking with her continues like this. I don't think my stress level can take the construction, detours and getting lost anymore.

I might as well answer her. "I really would have to say that this should be obvious by now. I've only been referencing them for the last week."

She feigns contemplation. She's probably remembering how I said walking through Times Square reminded me of Charlie in the tunnel in *Perks*

47

of *Being a Wallflower*. Maybe she's remembering my *Alice in Wonderland*-esque analogy. Perhaps it was the other 326 references I made. Either way, she says, "Let me guess. Does it have to with a stack of paper splashed with words set into binding?"

"Yes. Books are what make me happy."

"Okay," she starts. "Well, why? I mean, I only read the same few books over and over again because nothing else really interests me. Or am I just not looking in the right places?"

Now I know that I'm about to set a new record on my personal nerd scale if we continue talking about this, so I reply, "One, it's going to sound really stupid. Two, yes, you're probably looking in all of the wrong places. Three, ask me about something else."

Ava rolls her eyes and sits up to face me. "It's not going to sound really stupid if it gives me some insight as to who you are and what makes your world spin on its axis. You can't back out when I just dropped a bomb. Let's try this again, shall we? Why are books such a big part of your life?"

I roll up onto one elbow and begin to pick at the comforter for no real reason apart from avoiding eye contact. Maybe if I pretend like I didn't hear her, she'll just move on.

"Um, hello? Are you going to stare at that spot on the comforter or are you going to answer me? I'd prefer the answering me option, please," she teased.

"I don't know. It's just going to sound really ridiculous," I lament.

"Stop it. Look at me," she demands. "It's not going to sound stupid. Did you hear what I just rattled off? Just tell me."

Hesitation creeps in as it always does when I start to talk about myself. It's an eerie feeling knowing that someone else wants to share in what you enjoy. I take a breath as she lies back down and faces me. "Okay, well. I guess I love books because they invoke feelings that we didn't know we had. You can get excited or angry or amused or distraught sometimes all with in the span of a few chapters. It's living so many different lives you would never have imagined living from the time you pick it up until the time that you stop. It shows you all the possibilities just waiting for us out there. You become so attached to the characters and the story lines that you forget just how boring your life really is."

"Right, but you told me that you never do anything for yourself or take a chance on anything," she reminded me.

"I know. That's where the books and the movies come in," I justified. "It's why I'm an English Lit major. I don't have to take chances or give memorable speeches or do anything outside of my little bubble because all of the adventure and mystery and acts of chivalry are all waiting for me within the confines of a book or what I write in countless notebooks."

"Aw, you still write in notebooks? That's so cute! I figured everyone just double-clicked and went about their business that way."

"There's no need to poke fun of my Pilgrim-like tendencies. We all have our own little quirks," I defend. It feels good to talk about this with someone other than my parents. At school, people usually just glaze over when I start to talk about books and then quickly change the subject. Right now, I just feel...normal. Telling her all of this is nice. Just as I think just how nice it is, she sidles up next to me and places her hand on my chest. Uh, should I say something?

"I'm glad I'm getting to know who you are," she admits. How come she's the one who keeps saving us from awkward silences or blunders? "It makes it easier for me to assume you're not some serial killer or on the brink of kidnapping me."

"Whoa there. You're the one who has essentially kidnapped me the last few days. I have more reason to be worried than you do."

I can feel her smile against the fabric of my shirt. The conversation feels effortless with her and the snuggling feels more comfortable than it had with both Jenny and Marisa. I wonder what her previous relationships were like. Had there been more than just the one she mentioned? What were the guys like? I consider asking her about them, but think better of it knowing that might be like pulling the pin out of a grenade. I wasn't into the idea of an explosion, so we just continued to allow the music to fill up the room.

After two more songs, I realized that all of the songs were very mellow. They were the type of songs you lay back and relax to. I can feel her even breathing next to me and open my eyes to look down at her. Ava has a small smile etched onto her face. I can't help myself. I reach over and pull her face to mine. The feeling of her lips against mine causes fireworks to explode behind my eyes. It starts off sweet before becoming more intense. I roll onto my back and pull her tiny body on top of mine. She breaks free to change the music, but my lips continue their expedition towards her neck. The music changes tempo and her mouth finds mine once again.

"Wait, wait, wait," she breathes. "Didn't I say that I wasn't wanting to slide into home plate today?"

"Yeah, but you didn't say I had to play by the rules, now did you?" I smirk at her. I don't think I've ever smirked at or talked to a girl like that. I'll roll with it.

She mischievously smiles back and replies, "No, I didn't. Touché. All right, Ron Burgundy. I guess I will indulge in some afternoon delight."

Her lips are on mine again before I realize that she just made a reference to *Anchorman*. If she wasn't there before, then this girl is now most certainly inside the gates of my heart.

CHAPTER SEVEN

Ava

Well, that was certainly unexpected. Wonderful, but completely unexpected. Was he at all that confident in the last week or so? I don't think so. The mellow music was back on and it allowed me to concentrate on what we had talked about before we brought a Motley Crue song to life. He really was as sweet as pie. Everything he does and says is genuine. There's no act. As we lay there intertwined, I started thinking that I totally get it now. This poor kid is so shy because he never really lives out his own storybook. I break the comfortable silence of Snugglefest 2010 to tell him, "Okay, I totally get it. So, you're like Waldo."

"Excuse me? You mean like that guy in the puzzle books?"

"Yes, Waldo. When you need to look for him, you'll always find him lost in the pages of a book."

Kiernan looks at me with an amused expression. "I never thought about it like that, but it completely works."

Well, what can I say? I tend to make astute observations every now and again. It's not an everyday occurrence, but it's not like it's a rare find on a fossil dig. While I am figuratively patting myself on the back for that one, Kiernan repositions himself to be on his side so as to look at me. With one arm under my neck and the other over my side to allow his hand to trace my spine, he says, "Well, I'd rather be a Waldo than a puzzle missing its pieces," he suggests.

Whoa there, cadet. This was my time to make all of the awesome statements and shine like a star. He's trying to steal my thunder, yet I'm strangely intrigued to hear where this leads. "Yeah, I don't know what you're getting at. Do you have something to back that up or was I supposed to be so wowed that I'd just go down in flames?" I challenge.

"Well, no offense, but it's as if you're a puzzle. You expect people to piece you together, but you always hide the final pieces, which leaves no one to know what the final picture really looks like. You can see what it looks like on the box, but it's never the same once you complete it."

God damn it! He just won another round of philosophical thought. I'm really going to need to up my game after this. I contemplate that mind blow for a minute and say, "Fair enough. Although my evaluation of you was creative, yours was both creative and more accurate. Bravo. Now, let's get to learning all about one another."

We talked for hours that day. I told him about how brutal the winters can get in the Midwest and he told me what it was like during hurricane season in the South. He told me how he got 10 stitches in his hand the first and only time he tried to play baseball. The epic story of how I broke my arm attempting aerial acrobatics on a friend's trampoline shortly followed. I told him how my grandma can manage to tell you a story about something completely irrelevant to what you said to which he followed up with how his uncle can never manage to finish one. It went from silly to serious and back and forth. The more we talked, the more I began to genuinely enjoy his company. When the time called to eat, he gained a few points with his culinary skills. The kid knows how to whip up a delicious panini in a snap. Even though we added food, the talking rarely ceased.

Once the food was polished off, we got down to a round of Twenty Questions. Have you ever smoked weed? Me: obviously, him: of course not. How many relationships have you been in? Me: two legit tagged situations (the two others never got beyond "talking"), him: just two as well. Siblings? Both of us are flying solo. The conversation lasted until both of our voice boxes began picketing for less strenuous activity and the colors outside the windows changed from bright to dim. I walked him to the door and tugged his shirt to bring his lips to mine.

Although it was hard to deny the budding feelings he had for me that were shown in his eyes, we spent the next two months in each other's company almost every day. I didn't know what exactly it was about him that just made everything feel so easy. We spent afternoons in coffee shops talking about our love lives. I told him what happened with Kyle and how before him, Casey and I broke up because we hated each other. In turn, he told me how Jenny broke his heart after he had broken up with Leah for cheating on him. One day we found a spot in Times Square to people watch the visitors of the city and counted fanny-packs. Afternoons were lost to the countless number of art museums and galleries containing some of the world's most important works and some of the downright bizarre. A game of finding an interesting piece and then creating a story from what we saw was quickly becoming a favored activity.

Kiernan often took me to Strand Books on 12th Street to educate me on all that I was missing in the literary world. The two of us would wind up and down the monstrous shelves pulling out book after book. I would open to a random page, read the first paragraph I would see out loud and he would do the same in another book. There was where he told me how his favorite book was *Fear and Loathing In Las Vegas* by Hunter S. Thompson. Reading that book turned him off from ever wanting to experiment with drugs, which made me roar with laughter. When he told me how he wanted to be a writer, it was hard to act surprised. I always left that labyrinth (the place scarcely qualifies as a store) with a new book or three. Palahniuk, Vonnegut and Shan were names that I became familiar with. It became less about him sharing his world with me and more about me wanting to be able to hold a conversation about books with others.

In turn, I would drag him to 18 different record stores and a few times we even went to shows at the Southpaw in Brooklyn. He quickly learned the joys of Tokyo Police Club, the happiness of Something Corporate and to accept the knowledge that anything Jack White and Dave Grohl touch is pure genius. Kiernan bought my favorite New Found Glory album (when excluding their self-titled because it's unbeatable) *Coming Home*, Elton John's greatest hits and every album John Legend ever put out. When I described every reason why "The Wind" by Cat Stevens is my favorite song of all time, he asked to listen to it. Just as I did with books, he did with music. Conversation between went from "you don't know what you're missing!" to "what did you think of it?"

Kiernan and I learned the ins and outs of each other as we laughed over dinners of some of New York's finest food and cheap burgers at Shake Shack. There were nights where we would talk so late into the night that we found ourselves intertwined in the late morning light of the next day. We talked about the future and where we saw our lives going when strolling through the Financial District. It was a sad discovery that my birthday was February 17th and his was July 21st which meant we had already missed celebrating it this year. One night we even had a game night with Madison and some of her friends from school. After he had left, they remarked on how charming he was. He took me to see indie films that I would have never heard of if he didn't show them to me. There wasn't a part of the city that we left unexplored and I was happy to be with someone who has such a different perspective on everything.

One afternoon, I walked into the apartment from a solo exploration of a nearby record store (apparently Kiernan had some secret mission to go on) to find Madison on the couch swimming in waves of homework. "Still doing homework?" I inquire.

"No, I enjoy surrounding myself with my schoolbooks for fun. Maybe try and absorb the knowledge seeping from them, you know?"

"Well, I can see that school is making you all types of chipper." I state. "Do you want something to eat?

She doesn't even look up from her work. "Why? Do you?"

"No, I was just asking because I can see that you're going to be here for awhile and that you probably haven't eaten in awhile."

She puts down her pen and looks at me. "I'm sorry. Do I know you?"

"What?" I laugh. "I was just offering to ease your burden. I can see that you're stressed out and that I should help you out in any way that I can, especially since I haven't spent as much time with you as I should be. I have to help pay you back for letting me stay here in some way."

For a second, all she does is stare at me like I just tried to explain quantum physics to her. "You know what? I like what this kid is doing for you," she pointed out. Madison went back to focus intently on whatever she was working on.

"What do you mean?"

"Maybe you don't see it, but you're a lot less of a judgmental bitch since you two have been spending so much time together over the last two months. You're much happier and a lot less negative."

"Hey, I'm not a-" but I was cut off by the look she threw my way. "Okay, fine. Maybe I am. Was. Whatever. I don't know. He just sees the world in such a simpler way. He doesn't complicate things or overanalyze what isn't even there like I seem to do. He makes me want to be different. Oh my God. I am literally a walking cliché."

She peels her eyes away from her book and looks at me. "No, you're not. And trust me, it's working. I'll love you no matter what, but I think this is a good thing for you. Now, please leave my presence. I have to bang my head against this book and hopefully remember some of this dribble I'm writing out for my exam."

With that, she waves me out of the room as if she was a Hollywood A-lister and I was the hired help. I stand up and walk towards the door leading to the room I am merely borrowing from Leslie. Before I can cross the threshold, I heard Madison's voice from behind me suggest, "But if you wanted to bring me something delicious and nutritious in about an hour, I wouldn't turn it down."

I swivel towards her and announce that I will summon my inner Jamie Oliver for her and then walk into my room.

About an hour and a half later, I place my *Go Ask Alice* face down on the bed and decide to check on Madison. When I walk out of the room, she has moved from the couch to flat on her stomach on the floor. I feel awful that she is surrounded by books and completely overwhelmed with work. I begin to walk towards the kitchen to fix something for the both of us.

"How are you still doing homework?" I ask. "I've read a couple of chapters in a book, uploaded my new CDs to iTunes, taken a quick cat nap and you're still working. Jeez."

I open the fridge and scan the insides. There's nothing really left since both of us have managed to put off refilling it with sustenance. We should probably go do that tomorrow. As I make a mental list in my head, I hear Madison yell, "That's it!" I nearly jump out of my skin and turn to see her sitting up and staring like a mad woman at the work surrounding her.

"What the hell was that, Mad?" I shout as I turn to look in her direction.

She continues to stare at the textbooks and notebooks that have created a fortress around her. "This is a joke," she whines. "My brain is turning into the consistency of a 7/11 Slurpee and I'm going out of my mind. I can't take this shit anymore. Get ready. We're going out."

Well, this could go poorly. I walk over to where she's sitting and plop myself down Indian style across from her with the scholarly wall between us. I have to approach this calmly otherwise she'll turn into a Code Red situation. "Are you sure you want to do that? You seem pretty frazzled."

"Are you kidding me? I'm more than just frazzled. I'm about to go *Girl, Interrupted* over here. I need to go out and take my mind off of all of this," she wildly gestures to the surrounding mayhem and looks back at me. Okay, crazy eyes. She looks up at me, down at the textbooks and then back up to me. I feel like she's seconds away from pulling a Britney and asking me to go buy the necessary tools to shave her head so she doesn't have hair to pull out.

"Well, I would prefer it if you didn't do that, so I guess we can go out. Where are we going anyway?" I ask.

"There's some penthouse party in Tribeca that a guy from my Shakespeare Lit class is throwing. His dad owns some sports team or something. Who cares? The point is, there promises to be an abundance of alcohol and guys."

I know that she's smart and won't make bad choices if I decided to head out early, so I ask if it's alright if I bring a stowaway.

"Yeah, that's fine. I don't want you to be alone when I hit my stride."

All types of crazy and the girl still manages to knock out the funny lines. Madison stands up and stretches her body. Looking down at me sitting on the floor, she says, "I'm going to take a shower. Start thinking of what I should wear tonight. I want everyone to know I'm a single lady a la

Sasha Fierce." A few steps towards the bathroom and she turns towards me again.

"Wait, did I just hear you say that you were reading?"

I stand up and make my way towards her room to pick out clothing options. "Yeah, why?"

She looks at me quizzically and plainly states, "But you don't read books—not all the time, anyway."

"Well, Kiernan gave me some pretty good suggestions. I really underestimated how great reading and books can be."

I hate when she looks me up and down like I'm some crazy Jerry Springer guest that just revealed I was sleeping with my half-my-age stepson. Once she's had her fill, she points her finger at me and turns to walk back towards the bathroom again. "Yep. I'm baking that boy a cake."

Two hours later and we're on the top floor of an apartment building in Tribeca. The music is loud and the laughter contagious. People sit grouped on expensive couches and in clusters of folding chairs brought in for more people to sit on. In the far right corner of the main room there's a game of beer pong going on. Spectators are lining each side anticipating the winning or losing shot and either cheer or groan when the cup is missed. I'm taking this all in as two of my friends come up and hug me.

"You've been here how long and we're just now seeing you?" Sam asks as he releases me from a hug. "A little harsh, don't you think?"

Sam and Kylie are friends Madison and I met on a trip here my freshman year of high school. They were shopping at the same store we were and I noticed how cute Kylie's shoes were. Naturally, I had to compliment her and it just snowballed from there. They became close friends of ours and very hospitable hosts whenever we felt like a weekend getaway.

I hug Kylie and justify my absence from their lives by saying, "I just wanted this trip to be something different. Besides, some of our adventures aren't as fun as they used to be since the three of you are now legally allowed in those places."

Kylie chimes in and says, "I guess. What have you even been doing? Madison told us that you've just been hanging out but that she barely sees you. How does that even work? You live in the same apartment!"

I feel like I'm being made out to be the bad guy here and I'm going to be honest, I'm not playing that game today. For some reason, something just feels off. "Don't put it all on me. She's been really busy with school, so she's in her own little world. But I don't know. I've just been really seeing all of the things I've managed to overlook every time I come here."

"You still should have called us," Sam points out.

We all start to look around the room and make small talk about all of the people there. Both Sam and Kylie manage to have something negative to say about every other person we single out. It makes me wonder why I should even consider staying friends with them. I guess Madison was right. The more time I spent with someone who isn't so cutthroat, the more I realize how obnoxious I used to be. It was as if I thought others were beneath me when in all reality, none of us are Greek gods or goddesses. We shouldn't put ourselves on such pedestals.

I'm just about on a roll with a brand new breakthrough when Kylie cuts in and asks, "Hey, who's that guy? I've never seen him before."

She points across the roof so Sam's and my eyes can follow to where she's looking. When I focus on who she means, I notice that it's two girls talking to Kiernan. It makes me happy to see him being social instead of sitting alone. Granted, I told him when we got there that I wanted him to go meet people instead of sticking with me, but the fact that he did it is nice. It makes me feel like maybe he's not the only one who's caused some sort of change in someone.

"That's actually who I've been spending a lot of my time with," I say. "His name is Kiernan. We met on the day that I, well, that we both got here."

"Why are you spending time with him? He doesn't really seem like the gregarious type. He actually seems sort of awkward," Sam says. His tone and statements are starting to offend me. I really don't like what he's saying. What's going on with me?

"Yeah, he is, but it's a sort of endearing quality about him. He's leaps and bounds from what he was when we first met."

Kylie looks at me and puts her hands up. "Wait, hold on. You met him the first day you got here? That's the guy that's staying with that super hot model Madison slept with that has that Calvin Klein ad in SoHo?"

"Yeah, they're cousins."

Sam and Kylie look at each other and start to laugh. I'm really confused as to what is so amusing about this conversation. Did I miss something? Do they assume that I'm spending time with him because I'm performing some social norm experiment? I don't understand what's going on, but now I know that I don't like it.

"What's so funny?" I ask.

"There's no way that that guy right over there is related to a model," Sam retorts before the two of them continue to laugh. Now I'm just getting annoyed.

"You cannot be serious right now. He's actually pretty attractive. You're just factoring in his slight awkwardness to his physical appearance," I say defensively.

Kylie seems to think I'm making a joke. She asks, "Are you serious? Oh, come on, Ava. We've all seen that ad and that guy over there just doesn't live up to the family looks."

My annoyance seems to be skyrocketing because I can feel my face warming up and far too many rude remarks begin to mold themselves on the back of my tongue. There's no need to cause a scene. There's also no reason to really be speaking to these two anymore. I hold back as best I can and stick to honesty.

"That is completely shallow of the two of you. He's actually really great and if you'd stop focusing your standards solely on looks, you wouldn't be permanent singles. Good job, guys. I'm going to find Madison."

Phew, that felt good. I walk a safe distance away from them so they can't start something unnecessarily and stop to look around the room for Madison. She's ten or so feet away on a couch atop some guy's knee laughing like a fool. She looks up and spots me. I must have looked like smoke was coming out of my ears because she was next to me in what felt like seconds.

"Are you okay?" she asks. "We're here to have fun, so why do you look so mad?"

My eyes follow the path back to where the other two are standing and land back on Madison. "Nothing. I got snippy with Sam and Kylie and then sort of stormed off."

"Why would you do that? You love those two."

"I know, I know. I just feel like they're these really catty people and then they were really rude about Kiernan. I mean, they've never even met the guy! If they would just meet him, they wouldn't have those rude comments to say about him. Then I got all defensive and what the hell. Am I actually developing feelings towards him? This can't be happening. What's wrong with me?"

I grab her arm. She releases my grasp and pulls me a few feet away where only a few people stand. "Okay, Tyler Durden. Stop with the psychotic episode."

"Am I really crazy?" I look at her panicked. "Don't throw things like that at me."

She shakes her head. "No, sweetie. You're not crazy."

"I just don't know what the hell is wrong with me! Kylie pointed him out and he's standing over there talking to other girls and I mean, I'm the one who told him to go meet people and spread his newly grown social wings, but did I feel a twinge of jealousy? I think I might have. And then they were being just plain rude about him and I wanted them to know just how great he is!"

"Well, I don't know what to tell you," she sighs. "It's really just up to you to decide how you feel. No one is going to be able to tell you what to do about this, babe. Although I would definitely calm down in public. A spectacle is okay at home, but never in public. We both know that."

I let my chin fall into my chest. "I know, I'm sorry. I don't know what happened. One minute I was fine, the minute I'm about to be Mount St. Helen's."

"You'll figure it out. Don't worry about it, okay?" She grabs my cup and tosses it into the closest trash can. "Let's get you a new drink."

"Actually, I think I'm going to go. I really just need some time to myself." You know, to figure this mess of a life I have just freshly created.

How is it that we both divert our attentions to exactly where Kiernan is standing? That's such a lovely quality about best friends. You're always on the same page whether you want to be or not. "Do you want me to tell him that you've left?"

I shake my head. "No, it's fine. I have to start taking more responsibility for my life. I'll go over there and tell him. I'll see you later," I tell her and walk towards Kiernan.

CHAPTER EIGHT

Kiernan

"Hey, I'm going to go," she tells me.

My hand slips effortlessly around her waist as her hand lands between my shoulder blades. It feels easy and it's one of the simple joys in life. I ask her if she's okay and she assures me that she's fine, just a little tired. I offer to go with her, but she insists on my staying and enjoying my night. She tells me she'll call me tomorrow and leans in for just a quick kiss before walking away.

I didn't think anything of it the rest of the night. I know that that might sound awful, but there was no red flag that told me that something was wrong, so I just had a good time. Too good of a time seeing as I was out until four and was asleep until one in the afternoon. I guess there goes my being a fully functioning member of society for the day. I spent the rest of the day cleaning up around the apartment and catching up on some reading.

By the time night had come, I was excited to see Ava. Spending time with her was always so exciting. It was always interesting and there hadn't been a single moment when I was around her that I thought I would rather be somewhere else due to boredom. I was fiddling with my hair in the mirror when I heard a knock at the door. I open the door and see her looking intoxicating, even all bundled up. The best part is, I don't even think she tries to be because she probably has no idea just how wonderful she is to take in.

She walks in and asks, "Are you ready to make up for my being 80 years old last night?"

I shut the door and walk back towards the bathroom. "Sure. Just let me finish getting ready and grab my coat. It'll only take a minute."

"All right. I'll still be here."

I walk into my room to quickly grab my jacket. When I walk out just a few seconds later while putting on my jacket, I notice that she's staring at the ground. Is she staring at the ground or is she actually staring at something? I just cleaned earlier. There's no mess to behold.

"What are you-" I start. She continues to look down but puts up a hand to silence me.

"Is that a Nintendo 64?" she asks without looking up.

"Uh, yes," I respond as she walks next to the TV and the video game console.

"Excuse me, but how have I never seen this before? Better yet, how the hell have we never played it before?"

"Well, it's not like the debate over which console is better has ever come up between us," I say.

She leans down to look at what games are tucked away. When she sees what game is in the console itself, she just about explodes with happiness. "Holy shit! Super Smash Bros!"

Ava stands up and slips off one boot and then the other. She peels her charcoal peacoat off and tosses it onto the couch as she sits on the floor. After making sure everything was plugged in right, she turns on both the console and the TV. I'm still standing in the same place wondering what's going on. Weren't we just getting ready to go out? Why did she just take her coat and boots off? I'm very obviously missing something here.

"You can forget going out," she adds. "This city will always wait when it comes down to a battle royale on Nintendo."

Is this a joke? All I can do is stare blankly at the spot where she sits on the floor. I don't know of very many girls that would rather stay in and hang out with Mario instead of going out. I had no idea that girls like her existed in real life. Radiant, intelligent, humorous and now a Nintendo supporter. She manages to surprise me again and again. Ava must have felt my confusion because she looks over to where I'm still standing. Yes, I'm still in the same spot.

"What are you doing? We're playing this. I'm not kidding. Sit your ass down." She sounds like a drill sergeant. I remove the jacket and the shoes that have barely been on long enough to absorb the heat from my body and place them back in my room. By the time I come back out, she's already picked her character and is waiting for me to choose mine. I take the seat next to her and she offers me the controller.

"I should forewarn you," she begins. "I'm sort of a Nintendo champion."

"Is that so?" I ask. "Why is that?"

She shrugs. "Well, when your parents are both high paid lawyers and you've never had a bedtime because they're either gone or asleep, you have to get good at something. I considered being a hooker for awhile but it just didn't seem productive enough. Mario seemed much more exciting."

"You never told me that," I say.

"That I considered being a hooker?" She must have felt my gaze because she laughed and continued. "I'm kidding. You learn something new every day, right? There's today's Ava puzzle piece for you."

We play for about a minute when I ask, "Do you see them a lot?"

"Not really, but it's made this relationship of ours quite nice. They put money in my bank account and I show up at events when they need the picturesque family moments for."

She seems unfazed by this topic. It's such a strange thing for me to encounter. That's not to say that all of my friends have the greatest relationship with their parents, but to be so distant from the people that brought you into this world is such a bizarre idea. How do you deal with that? For the next few minutes, the only noise in the room is the clacking of the controllers and the music from the video game.

While we wait for the next level to load, she asks me what my parents are like. I tell her that they're just like me. They're introverted nerds who teach college philosophy and European history. It was a match made in honor roll heaven. My dad likes to paint and my mom is a fan of the piano.

They're also just like me in the sense that they too have spent all of their lives in North Carolina. They're very polite in that Southern way and incredibly happy with the way that their lives have turned out so far.

"Well, kudos to them," she offers. "They obviously raised you to be a Southern gentleman. It's really quite an endearing and refreshing quality of your personality. I'd like to high five them for that."

I didn't want to tell her that they would probably look at her like she was nuts if she was all excited about giving them a high five for raising their children the exact same way that they were raised. They would end up laughing uncomfortably and pretend to drop something on the floor. She didn't need to know that.

"I'm seriously killing you right now, Kiernan."

We allow the intensity of the game silence us so as to give our full attention to the game. Both of us are making noises that we assume will help our game when in reality just make us look like idiots. A few more minutes of playing and Ava's hands go in the air as I drop my controller to the floor.

"Yes! That's right!" she triumphantly yells. "I won! I told you I would defeat you and look at that! I totally did."

"The only reason you won is because this old controller's B button sticks."

"Yeah, I'm sure that's it," she sarcastically says. "It has nothing to do with my superior skill, right? Nothing but excuses out of you. How about we try again? It's not like you'll win, but that's not really the point."

Her shoulder nudges into mine and we start another game. Of course she beats me again. I have to remember to not tell my friends that. It can ruin my gaming reputation. By the next game, I decide it's okay to ask her to elaborate on the situation with her parents. If she so easily mentioned the fact that they're not close earlier, she might tell me more about it. I can't get the idea out of my mind that they don't play that big of a part in her life.

"So, what's the deal with you and your parents?" I offer.

"What do you mean?" she asks.

"Well, you basically said the three of you lead separate lives. What do you mean?"

Ava tells me that her parents are very serious about their work. They started their own firm just a few years after getting married and graduating law school. When her grandparents pestered her parents about having children, they had Ava. Having a child and being as busy as they were proved to be extremely difficult, so they never had any other children. Her winning sarcasm and gift of charm were consequences of not having anyone around to tell her no.

"Nannies can only do so much for kid," she told me. "Then they want their parents and what is the nanny supposed to do? Anyway, when I met Madison, things just got easier. Her parents were both pretty busy, too. We learned how to get what we want and how to entertain people. Sure, it hurt the two of us that our parents never really wanted to spend as much time with us as parents should or really reprimand us for our poor choices, but you live and you learn. I know that they love me and I know they worry about my safety and whatever, but I do sometimes wish things were different. I wish I was able to be more open with people, but what can you do? You just accept it and move on. You learn what you don't want to do when you have your own kids one day."

After that, I wasn't quite sure what to say. She didn't offer up anything else in regards to it and I didn't ask her to. We play for almost five hours by the time we realized our eyes can't take staring at the screen anymore and our hands felt like carpal tunnel is about to set in. We lay down on the couch and talked about anything that came to mind until we fell asleep and the next thing we know it's the morning. Travis must have purposely dropped the controller to make a noise because, well, he's a jerk and would do something like that.

"Rise and shine, kiddies."

I can hear him fall into the chair since my eyes still haven't adjusted to waking up just yet. Ava asks what time it is as we untangle our limbs. Of course we don't get a straight answer from him, but instead something about it being time to get a watch. He's so original.

"No, really. What time is it?" I ask.

He takes a bite out of the banana in his hand before he tells us that it's just after 7 AM. Well, I guess I'm not that mad about his attitude now. That is far too early for anyone to be in a chipper mood.

Ava stands and says, "I should get going. I don't even remember falling asleep." She pulls on her boots, looks at Travis and asks, "Wait, why are you just getting in?"

"Well, if you must know, I had a fitting last night for a photo shoot I have next week and it got turned into going out drinking and then sleeping with the stylist for the shoot."

"You are such a class act, you know that?" she quips.

"You know, I do know that. I have medals and trophies for how awesome I am. I understand that you are in awe of someone such as myself. It's okay. Bask in the glory of being in my presence. I'll allow it."

Ava looks at me and we both roll our eyes. I love the guy, but he is truly an arrogant prick. She pulls on her coat and asks if I'm going to walk her to the door. I open the door for her and she stands on the tip of her toes to give me a small kiss.

"Thanks for last night. I think it was a lot better than going out," she tells me before turning and walking down the hall to the elevator. I look at her one more time and shut the door. Still too tired to do much else, I walk back to the couch and sit down deep in the cushions. Travis starts to laugh and I really can't understand why. He thinks his game is so good that he might as well have invented the sport.

"What?"

"Nothing, man," he laughs. "The sex just must have been pretty good."

I look at him affronted. "We didn't have sex last night. Not every friendship or whatever the hell this is has to involve sex. There are other things that are more important. Have the flash bulbs made you forget that? Should I be concerned?"

"I forgot how funny you weren't. And I doubt that. You guys had to have had sex."

We could have sat there and gone back and forth all day with this. He seriously couldn't understand that all we did was hang out and play Nintendo. The fact that we talked as well didn't seem to register with him. He was just astonished that instead of going out, we sat in with Mario all night.

"It was better than going out. Especially since she left the party the other night about an hour after we got there."

"Whoa, wait. You stayed at that party the other night without her?"

"Yes. Why? Am I not allowed to do that?"

Travis feigns concern. "No, you just never stay at places alone apart from any place that has books and you never even last at parties for ten minutes, let alone an entire night."

"You do know people can change, right?"

"Yeah, I see that. I really think it's because of that girl that you've changed. She's like Pocahontas. She's transferring her outgoing spirit onto you."

I shake my head and point out that I don't think that's how that whole process works, but I definitely commend him on trying out some new material to get his point across. He really seems to be branching out lately and I like that. Standing up and stretching, Travis announces that he's going to get some sleep and recommends that I get a bit more because not everyone has the ability to wake up and look as good as he does at any point in the day. Such a charmer that boy is.

Before he can go, I tell him that I've been talking with my parents and I've already applied for a transfer to Columbia starting either next semester or the following fall. I've thought it through and it just seems right. It seems like a good idea and the English program, along with the school itself, is really great. Being here can really help elevate my writing since there's so much to draw inspiration from. Although none of that matters to him, the fact that I had an ulterior motive did not manage to escape his attention.

"You spend a few months with that girl and all of a sudden you want to be adventurous. I've been trying to get you out of that turtle shell your whole life. That sex really must be magic or I'm sort of hurt."

"Yes, I'm sure you are. And the sex has nothing to do with it. She just made me see the possibilities in life. I haven't even told her that I've been doing this and that it was now just a matter of waiting to hear back from the admissions office."

Travis contemplates this bit of information and adds, "Is that your way of asking me if you can live with me if you get in? Tell me your big secret? Because if it is, I'm going to have to write up a rules sheet for you. And yes, that's my way of saying that you can mooch off of me and the good fortune my good looks have given me."

Walking back towards his room, I very audibly mention how he can be such a nice guy when he wants to be.

"Yeah, don't get used to it. I plan on not turning down the noise when I have a girl staying over. You should just know that now."

He shuts his bedroom door and all I can do is laugh. My life has been changing left and right and not one second of it has scared me. It's liberating to embrace the inevitable or intentional changes in your life. Moving here permanently will provide so many necessary changes that I'm actually elated to tackle head on. I think I'm starting to get a little delirious. I think it's time I get some more sleep.

CHAPTER NINE

Ava

The last few days have been so nice. I don't mean the weather, because it's almost winter in New York City. It's nice to see the city change with the seasons but still stay the same. Let's add that one to the list of reasons this city is so great. It's also been nice to just mosey around by myself at times. I spent all of Tuesday just walking around the Museum of Natural History by myself. It was fun, but right now is not one of the times where I want to spend time alone. I've called Kiernan a few times to see if he wants to grab something to eat, but I get no answer. Oddly enough, I'm not too far from their building. I'll just go see if he's there. Maybe his phone just died or something.

I'm walking down their street when I hear my name. I look around for the source of this and wonder if they're not calling to someone else. Rarely have I met someone who shares my name, but it's a possibility. To my right, I see Travis as he trots up the street to see me. Odd. I didn't know the two of us were on a "let's shout each other's names down the block" basis. Being the friendly type that I am, I give him a hug and say hello. Apparently he's just come back from a go-see and asked if I was going to his place.

"I was, actually. I wanted to see if Kiernan wanted to go grab some food or something. He's not answering his phone, so I figure I would just stop by since I was in the area."

"Well, he's not there," he explains. "He headed out around 10 and said he wanted to go look around some museum or something. Don't quote me on that, because I wasn't really listening. Anyway, you're more than welcome to come up, if you'd like. Hang out until he gets back or whatever."

Why am I getting some weird feeling about this? You know the type of feeling you get before you realize something is a really bad idea? That's the type of feeling I've got brewing. I'm not sure why. It's not like this kid is dangerous in any way. I'm probably just paranoid about absolutely nothing. Besides, what else did I have to do? Oh, right. Nothing. I might as well.

We walk into the building and take the elevator to their floor. We walk in and he throws his keys on the counter. We both take off our coats and toss them over the side of the couch. Suddenly I'm extremely curious about his life. I've managed to speak to him only a handful of times and I'll be honest, they weren't the most riveting conversations I've had in my life. Getting to know him seems like a good idea and I'm bored. We might as well go for a round of 20 Questions. Why is that bad feeling there again?

"So, I don't think I've ever asked you, which is strange since I never shut up, but do you like being a model?"

"Well, we can't all be surgeons and accountants. Someone had to step up and take one for the team and become the eye candy." Damn, that smile really is perfect for a toothpaste ad. Whatever brand he's hawking, I'm buying. Wait, what? Focus, girl. Focus on something else other than those full lips and...no. Witty comment. Give a witty comment!

"You also wear the jersey for the cockiest, too. You should be given a sash or something for all your help."

Victory is mine! The two of us start to laugh. He walks into the kitchen and asks if I would like something to drink. Is he nuts? I've been walking around New York City. Of course I'd like something to drink. He grabs two beer bottles out of the fridge and takes the caps off both before handing one to me. I don't think he answered my question, though. If he keeps talking, I don't have time to center my attention on his sculpted biceps. Really, self? Stop that!

"Thank you. You should probably answer my question," I point out.

"Oh, right. Yeah, I like it. It's fun and I get to go to a lot of pretty cool places and meet some really successful people. It can get pretty catty sometimes, but the whole thing is a rush."

"Well, as long as you like doing it. That's all that matters." And just like that, we've lapsed into an awkward silence. Thank God this is a beer and not a Hawaiian Punch he gave me. I'm unsure of what to do or say next, so I resort to fussing with my hair. That always seems to keep me occupied and forget that that creepy feeling is still hanging out in the pit of my stomach. Before I can dive deep into why it might be there, Travis starts talking again.

"You know, he really cares about you."

Tell me something I don't already know, GQ. He tells me that he talks about me quite often and that I should be careful. Are you my mother? Please. But just to be on the safe side, I ask why I should be so careful and Travis tells me that there's a good chance that Kiernan will form a solid attachment to me. Do I want that? I'm already conflicted as it is with my feelings. This little pow-wow isn't helping me sort anything out. If anything, it's making it worse. I can't let on that I'm conflicted. I just need to sound reasonable and tell the truth to the best of my ability.

"Well, he knows that I'm nowhere near wanting anything serious. Yeah, I do care about him, but it's not like that. Plus, I have no intention of staying here which puts us again in two separate places. So, that sounds like it's kind of a personal problem for him."

"I hope he does know that," Travis says. "If I have to hear one more time about how soft your lips are, I might have to dropkick him down Fifth Avenue."

"Hey, now. I was just born with luscious lips. I can't be held accountable for that."

I'm sorry, but did it just get awkward in here? I feel like it might have permeated the air really quick. That was definitely an awkward giggle that erupted from my mouth. Speaking of my mouth, why did he have to bring up my kissing expertise? Why is he looking at me like that? And now he's moving towards me. Great. What the hell do I do? He closed the space between us in about two steps and is now cupping my face in his hand. His thumb feels smooth as it slides along my bottom lip. Should I warn him that I carry a rape whistle? Good God, he's tall.

"So, if you're not looking for anything serious, it wouldn't matter if I do this."

Travis leans down and gently places his lips on mine. Oh my God, that kiss felt like heaven. His mouth doesn't even taste like the beer that I watched him drink. It tastes like a welcoming party's appetizer before the meal that welcomes me to town. He pulls back and my eyes start swimming with stars. What did he say? Something about me not wanting something serious? He's right. I don't want that and why isn't he kissing me again? I don't even realize that I'm staring at him with my jaw halfway to the floor. Was I supposed to say something?

"No, I don't think it matters," I tell him.

That smile is a lethal weapon, I swear. He leans down and kisses me again. His tongue slides into my mouth and it takes all of my strength to not devour him whole. The intensity increases and the height difference starts to hinder the fun. I move to pull off his shirt as he starts to walk us back to his room. Where did my top go? I didn't even notice it was gone. Travis picks me up with what seems like no effort and my legs wrap around his torso. I hear the door slam behind us as we fall to the mattress and I'm dizzy from his kiss alone.

CHAPTER TEN

Kiernan

I walk into a dark apartment. I thought Travis was supposed to be home by now. Hmm. He must still be out. I flip on the light switch and make my way to the kitchen to plug my phone in. It must not have charged overnight because it died about ten minutes after leaving this morning. I didn't have time to run back since I had a meeting with an advisor from Columbia. I notice that Travis's phone is already plugged into my charger. The phone is almost charged. When I go to unplug it, I see that he has a voicemail from Ava. Now, I'm not naturally a snoop, but I'd have to admit that I was interested in what she could possibly have to say to him. I mean, they've only met a few times. Besides, smart phones just make it too easy to listen to voicemails.

"Hey, it's Ava. Listen, today was a really big mistake. That sounds rude, but I don't really care. It was a really bad idea. Can we agree to not tell him that we slept together? That'd be great. Thanks. I'll talk to you whenever."

I'm sorry. What? What the hell just happened? There's no way I heard what I did. There's no way she could have done that. Not to me, at least. I grab the phone and find the nearest chair to play the message back one more time and realize I wasn't imagining what she said. I know that we never really talked about being exclusive or whatever but is this a joke? With him? What was the series of events that could have even lead to that? And, since time has a tendency to do this to you, it's just then that Travis walks out of his room wearing only a pair of basketball shorts and asks me why I look a little bit out of it.

"Did you...did you really sleep with her?" I can't even bring myself to look at him right now. I'm lucky that I managed to ask that as calmly as I did. If he did sleep with her, that level of calm will quickly vanish.

"What are you talking about, man? I sleep with a lot of girls. You have to be a little more specific."

Who the hell else would I mean? I can feel the anger rising in my voice as I try my best to contain it. "Ava. Did you really sleep with her?"

Well, I threw him a curve ball on that one. He mulls over how best to answer that question as he leans back against the kitchen counter and crosses his arms. Why does he look so amused? This isn't funny.

"How would you have even found out about that?"

I'm so happy that he didn't even deny it. Then I could really stay mad at him for lying to me. I don't even need to ask if he did or if he didn't. He wears his conquests around like they're gold star stickers for good work. He could tell exactly what I was thinking. It was written all over my face and was seeping out of my body.

"Yeah, so what? It's not like you're together and she didn't exactly say no."

I'm on my feet and shaking my head at Travis. "How could you do that to me? You know exactly how I feel about her!"

He doesn't even move. He continues to lean back with that stupid smirk on his face. "Exactly. That's why I did it. I seized an opportunity to show you that you can't just run around falling for some pretty girl that gives you attention. If she cared about you as much as you care about her, she would have said no. Besides, it was something I wanted and I took it."

"Are you fucking kidding me?" Oh, using that word is new. "What the hell is wrong with you?"

"Nothing is wrong with me. Lighten up, okay? I did you a favor." Travis stands up to speak to me at eye level. "She doesn't want to date you, so you might as well get that stupid idea out of your head now. She was free game. You'll come to realize this and then get over it."

He pats me on the shoulder and walks back into his room. What do I do or even say right now? Being of the violent nature would serve me well right now. Instead, I kick the leg of the chair I was just previously sitting in and run my hands through my hair. I sit back down with my elbows on my knees and my head in my hands. I sit like this for a few seconds before I cross the room to plug my phone in. While I wait for it to turn back on, I think about everything that just happened. Sure, Travis was right but did he need to go to such extremes to prove that to me? Why did she do that to me? Is she back to being the person who doesn't care about other people's feelings? I hear the phone turn back on and search for her number. The phone rings once, twice and she picks up.

"Oh, hey. What's up? I tried to get a hold of you earlier but your phone was dead or something."

It sounds like she's trying to force sounding cheerful and not give herself away. That's not going to help the situation. I've never had to deal with this situation so for a second, I let her statement hang in the air while I figure out what to say next. I should have thought about what I was going to say to her beforehand. All right. It's best to just say it right off the bat.

"Right. Was that before or after you slept with my cousin?"

It goes so silent between us that I check my phone to make sure that she hasn't hung up. I'm not even questioning my bluntness. If you want answers, you need to ask questions. I'm acting like an adult about this so now it's her turn to be one and admit to what happened. If she can't admit to what happened, then it's not even worth trying to talk about.

"Kiernan, I'm sorry. I-"

I don't even let her finish what she probably thought up to say in the event that I do find out. "Sorry? Sorry? Well, that just seems pretty meaningless. If you were sorry, you wouldn't have done it in the first place."

"Can we just get together and talk about this?"

Is she out of her mind? I don't even want to see her right now. I don't necessarily want to see Travis either, but with that one, I don't really have a choice. "Yes, that sounds like a real treat. We can get ice cream and talk about how great everything is. Yeah, right."

"Why are you being like this?" I can hear the hurt in her voice. I know she can hear it in mine.

"I don't know, why did you do it? Actually, don't answer that. I really have no desire to speak to you."

"Kiernan, are you serious? It was a mistake!"

I tell her, "Saying it was a mistake doesn't take the sting out of it. Forget it. I'll see you around," and press the end button. I wish I knew better how to deal with this type of situation. Normally I would talk to Travis about this but that card left the table. Why did I have to listen to that voicemail? It could have just been her calling to see why I wasn't answering my phone. I should have just assumed that was it and moved on. I didn't need to be a snoop. At the same time, if I hadn't heard that voicemail, would either one have ever told me? I can't think about this here. I need to go out and clear my head. I grab my jacket, head out the door and slam it behind me.

CHAPTER ELEVEN

Ava

I haven't left the apartment since he hung up on me. My iPod has been on the same album. I'm finding it easy to space out and not realize I've been looking at the same thing for 25 minutes. I barely register the fact that Madison has walked into the room and sat down next to me. I think she might have asked me a question, but I'm not really listening. Did she just say something about my not leaving for the last three days? Or was it about my being lost in thought? Oh well. I don't really need to talk about it. My headphone cord moves and I deduce that she has picked up my iPod. I feel her pull the cord until an ear bud falls out. I guess that means she wants to talk to me.

"The Avett Brothers? When were you going to tell me that I would no longer be graced with your presence? Or were you just going to leave in the dead of night?"

I pull my attention away from staring at nothing in particular to look at her and force a smile. "You know, I really need to stop letting my musical selections betray me. I was going to tell you today because I'm leaving tomorrow afternoon."

Madison seems confused. "But the semester isn't over yet. What are you going to do for the next two weeks?"

"That's an excellent question, Miss. What am I going to do? I haven't put much thought into it. I don't really care, to be honest. There's just no point in my staying here anymore, despite how much I've loved spending time with you since you thought it was okay to leave me to move here."

"Look, just stay until the semester breaks for Christmas," she pleads. "You can't just run away from whatever happened in your head to make you want to leave."

I place my hand on top of hers. "Oh, I'm not running away. I've just learned all that I could have hoped to. I'm running back to who I know I should probably be and I don't think that I'm going to be able to do that here."

We sit in silence and figure out what I mean. I'm just as lost as Madison is as to what I just said, but there's no need to tell her that. The confusion I feel is my own and I don't really think anyone can help me sort it out. The only thing that both of us gather from what I've said is that my decision to leave is final. When I decide the time is up, I can't be shaken.

Madison pulls her hand out from mine and says, "Fine. I guess I have to accept your decision. Although, I can't accept that you haven't showered. You're starting to smell like a frat house and it's messing with the fresh floral scent I like my apartment to maintain."

"You know, I was thinking of continuing this." I gesture towards the hoodie and yoga pants I've been in for the last few days. "It gives me some bonus time in the day that showering took up. Plus, isn't the government complaining that we're always using too much water? Seriously, the positives to this keep adding up," I jest.

"Yeah, as much as I would enjoy the myriad of sarcastic banter we could throw around like a dodgeball with this, I'd like it if we could just skip to the part where you said you were getting in the shower."

Laughing as I haul myself off of my little island of misery, I feel a small pain of sadness that this type of conversation will regress back to technological communication instead of face to face. Instead of her being able to judge by my expression that she's victorious, I'll have to spell it out for her. It's hard when you grow up thinking nothing will ever change and then you get separated from those you love and realize even the smallest things such as being able to look someone in the eye when you're talking to them means the most.

I start my slow stroll towards the bathroom when I hear her say, "Thank you. And when you're done, you should probably call him." I turn back to face her so she knows that I'm listening. "He deserves to know you're leaving and you need to say something about whatever happened between the two of you. I don't need to know the specifics to know that you probably owe him an apology. You're slipping into the early stages of senility if you think you didn't crack that kid's heart just a little bit."

It seems to me that she's the one that's always right. Whenever you're wrong, you know that in the back of your head, she's the voice that you hear saying, "I told you so." Talking to him about it is one of the only things I've been able to think about the last few days. I know I have to do it. I consider walking over to hug her but then I remember the state that my outer appearance is in and think the better of it.

"I know. I'll call him tomorrow morning. That's pretty late notice but I need to figure out what I need to say first."

She grabs a magazine off the couch, opens it and props her legs on the edge of the coffee table. "I'll add it to the list of great advice I've given you and bill you later."

I shake my head and walk into the bathroom. I turn the water on, close the lid to the toilet and take a seat. What am I going to say? Moreover, what could I possibly say to make this sound okay to him? I know it's not okay, but I guess I wonder what I can say to make it okay between the two of us. Why did I even do what I did? I don't know if I was trying to prove that I was in fact single and not attached or what. Was it impulse or was it stupidity? I guess some people associate one with the other, so it could be both, but even with that conclusion I don't think it fits. Steam starts to filter out from behind the shower curtain. My thoughts are just as cloudy as the mirror starts to become. I don't know what I'm going to say tomorrow. I just know that I have to make this right.

CHAPTER TWELVE

Kiernan

It's been four days since I found out what happened. I've been avoiding Travis as much as possible and have had no contact whatsoever with Ava. There have been a few brief moments when I've thought to pick up the phone and call her, but this isn't my mistake to fix. If I just go running back, she'll assume that this is okay to do to anyone and it's not. My phone starts to vibrate on the table. It rings twice, three times before I pick it up to see who the caller is. Great, it's Ava. Again, I'm doing my best to maintain the maturity to handle my problems that my parents brought me up to have, so I answer.

"Hi. I know that I'm probably the last person you want to hear from right now, but please don't hang up. I need to speak to you." Her voice sounds small and defeated. If this were any other conversation, I feel like this would have been used as a ploy to get me to do something I didn't want to. Unfortunately, this is not one of those times, so I'm lead to believe that it's all genuine emotion. I tell her that I suppose the two of us could talk and she asks if I could meet her in Washington Square in about 10 or 15 minutes. I certainly can't guarantee that time frame, but I do tell her I'll meet her there before we end the phone call.

I continue to sit there for a minute before I reluctantly get up. I grab my phone and bundle up to avoid getting sick from this cold weather. How appropriate, right? Cold weather or rain seems to occur conveniently in troubled times. I shake my head and exit the apartment building shortly after and make my way towards the Village to meet her. It would have been nice if she could have chosen a place for us to meet that was, I don't know, indoors. That would have been nice of her. All right, I need to stop being so negative. The fact that she even called me, or wants to talk face-to-face, seem like a few huge steps.

I think about things that she might say and what I could say back. I want to be stern and aloof but that makes me look like a complete tool. I also don't want to hurt her feelings because this is probably hard for her to deal with. I continue bouncing back and forth between what I want to say and then I'm in Washington Square. I look around until I spot her looking down in her lap and fiddling with her gloves on a bench on the other side of the park. For a split second, I consider turning around and going back the way I came. Too bad that would make me look like a asshole. I don't want to be like that. Instead, I skeptically walk to the bench where she's sitting. I stop a few feet away and wait until she looks up to see that I'm there. Thankfully, it doesn't take her long. The smile she gives me is not only faint but seems apologetic. She pats the seat next to her and I sit down, leaving a gap between us.

"How are you?" she asks.

I'm fantastic. How does she want me to respond to that? "Fine," I say. Man-of-few-words mode has returned.

"That's good."

It seems like a good idea to make small talk so we can actually speak to one another instead of sitting here staring off in different directions. "I applied to Columbia."

She spins towards me. "What?! That's great! Why didn't you tell me?"

"Well, I was meeting with the advisor when you couldn't get a hold of me the other day and then...you know."

This is going well. We've already had awkwardness, a high and then a low. All within the span of about thirty seconds. For both of our sakes, I hope that this conversation gets easier because I don't like how uncomfortable and forced this all seems. We sit there for a second before she says, "Look,

I'm really sorry that I hurt you. I really am, but beyond that, I'm not entirely sure what you want me to say to you."

I shake my head and look the other way. What do I even want her to say to me? That she was wrong? That she feels so bad that she'll do anything to make it up to me? That I'm the only one for her? I don't even know. Her hand tugs on my arm and she asks me to talk to her. She tells me what I had already suspected about admitting to this mistake and wanting to fix it. It doesn't necessarily make me feel any better, but knowing that this is hard for her, makes it easier for me to hear her out. I figure now would be the time to insert my own thoughts.

"I'm not sure why you did it and frankly, I don't want to know. Yes, it hurts a little bit more because of who it was with because I sort of live with him, but I can't really do much about that. What confuses and hurts the most is how you could do that to me. Don't you care about me at all?"

"Of course I do! How can you even ask me that?"

I consider for a second not saying what I'm about to say. This could change the dynamic of our relationship. Do I even want to risk that once we patch all of this up? No, I can't second guess myself. She just told me that she cared about me, right? I have to be a big kid about this. I twist my body to face hers and say, "Don't you know that I love you?"

Instead of looking at me like I was crazy or getting up and walking away, she looks down and pulls my hands into hers before placing them in her lap. "I do know that. I really do. And you have to know that I love you, too. It's just not in the way that you want it to be."

"What do you mean?"

"The love that you're looking for me to give you is the kind of love that involves white picket fences and all of that happily-ever-after hoopla."

So, she loves me but doesn't? I'm so confused. "So, you're trying to tell me I'm like a brother? That's...kind of weird."

She smiles and admires the shape our hands clasped together makes. What else could she mean? Even when I'm mad at her, hurt by what she's done, and confused by whatever it is she's trying to say to me, all I want to do is reach over and run my hand along her jaw line. I know that that would be inappropriate, but it's all I can think about doing. Well, that and figuring out what she's trying to tell me.

"No, not like a brother," she says. "I had no idea what I expected to get out of this little excursion of mine. I wasn't sure what I was looking for, but you waltzed right on in to show me. That's why I brought you here. I wanted to tell you that I was going home. I mean, I had to leave in a few weeks anyway when Leslie came home. I'm just jumping the gun a little bit."

Okay, that's not what I was anticipating. I look her in the eyes to see if she was serious. I shake my head in the hopes that it will take what she said and change it. How could she be leaving? I'm a mix of shock and confusion. I don't even know what to say. All at once, the questions flew from my mouth.

"I don't get it. Why would you leave? What could I have given you that is so easy to give up? Why can't you just stay here?"

Suddenly I'm not even upset about what happened. I'm upset that this wonderful human being will no longer be within the same city limits as me. Granted, with the technology of today, it won't be hard to continue speaking to one another, but there's no longer just a train or cab ride between us. It turns into $300 and airport security. I'm lost in that idea before she brings me back.

"Probably because it was never about changing the location on the map of my life. I just needed someone to help me straighten out the highway lines to lead me in the right direction. That's what you did for me. You showed me that you need to stop and look at the scenery instead of always focusing on what the next stop is. That's why the love I have for you is so special. It can never be matched. No one could ever do for me in my life what you have done for me in the short time we've known one another. It probably sounds cheesy, but don't you think that that might just be better than what you want from me?"

Everything that she's saying to me makes her leaving hurt even more. I don't want to look at her in the eye because this conversation is already too emotionally charged. I don't think we need physical evidence of it as well. There's so much that I want to say to her but I fear that whatever it is that comes out will come out all wrong. The words swim through my head and yet no response seems good enough to give her. I clear my throat and make do.

"You're right," I tell her. "I do want the white picket fence business with you. As hard as it is to know that that could never happen, the type of love that you just described is even rarer." I hesitate before I continue. "I could never put into words how much you've changed me and how much you will always mean to me, so there's no hope in trying."

We both sit and look at our hands still clasped together. Even though she has been breaking my heart and even though I got a little frantic, our hands stayed just as they were. Each of us has both the same and completely different things to let soak in. We both felt that the time was coming to a close. Ava pulls her hands out from mine and stands up to place a kiss on the top of my head. She begins to walk away and before she can get too far, I run to catch up to her. I pull her close and hold tight to remember the mold of her body against mine. When we slightly break apart, I kiss her with as much love as I can muster and hope it translates. She looks up at me and hugs me as she whispers a thank you into my jacket.

Ava breaks away from me and walks back to the street that will lead her back to the apartment building where she no longer resides. I watch her back as she reaches the crosswalk because I'm unable to move. Before she walks out of my line of vision, she steals one last look at me and smiles. Even though I'm a wreck on the inside, her smile is infectious and I find myself smiling as well. She vanishes from my sight and I shake my head as I walk in the opposite direction. I know that we changed one another. I know that our paths in life crossed for all the right reasons. As I walked away with no particular direction in mind, my inner hopeless romantic had hope that one day would instead be the right time.

CHAPTER THIRTEEN

Ava

When I detached my arms from the circle they made around his waist, it was all I could do to just walk away and not send a glance back his way. I had to stare straight ahead and pretend that I couldn't feel his eyes burning holes in my back or the shape of his lips on mine. By the time I had reached the street and hailed a cab, I was wondering what I was doing. Before I jumped in the cab that would take me back to my belongings and subsequently to the airport so I can head back to my new reality, I paused and allowed myself a look back at him. Would he still be looking at me? Or would he be lost amongst all of the other patrons?

I looked directly behind me and saw that he was still standing there with his hands tucked inside the front pockets of his jeans. Kiernan looked both defeated and hopeful all at once. It was such an interesting contortion of his features that smiling seemed so natural when I looked at him. The smile that spread across his face in return was instantaneous. It suddenly became difficult to want to place myself in the back of the car instead of running back towards his embrace. I knew right as the thought entered my mind that I had to get into the car or I would rethink my decision and wind up staying. Knowing that would put back my progress, I quickly got in the cab and gave the address to the driver.

The cab eases itself into the flow of traffic and the noise can't seem to get by the do not disturb sign I thought I had placed on the thoughts that I was having. What am I even doing? Is what I said to him even the whole truth? Yes, I do love him, but why do I feel like it might just be the real deal instead of what I threw out there? I was so sure that it wasn't this morning, but now I can't seem to get the idea out of my head. I think about the warmth of his body, the way his eyes would light up whenever something amused him and his eager curiosity to learn something new. I remember the way his hand seemed to be molded for mine and how it always reminded me of the song "I Was Made for You" by She & Him.

The scent of his skin and the shape of his smile start to cloud my mind and suddenly I realize the driver is speaking to me. I realize we're back in front of the apartment building, apologize and decide it's a better idea to get another cab later. If Madison is still home, she'll want to know what happened. I quickly reach the apartment and place the key in the lock for the last time. I look around and feel a wave of homesickness for it already. Seriously? I haven't even left yet. I shake the feeling away and walk towards the room I had occupied to pack my bags. Madison must have heard me come in because when I turn around, she's leaning against the doorway biting her lip.

"What?" I ask.

"Well, I just wanted to know how it went. That's all," she says.

How did it go? How do I answer that? I don't even know how it went and I was there. Now I'm the one biting my lip and what's the phrase? Furrowing my brow? I'm pretty sure that's it. Yes, I'm furrowing my brow and trying to figure out how to go about telling her this story. Should I tell her about my confusion with my feelings? I mean, she already knows that, but it's on a different level now. Maybe she'll be able to help me with that now.

"Are you okay?"

I snap my head up to look at her. "What? Me? Yeah. It's just that I'm not exactly sure how I feel about all of it."

"How about you give it a try as we try to pack the massive amount of clothes you own?" She moves from the doorway to sit on the edge of the bed where I've made a mountain of fabric. "I really didn't think we shopped that much, but there's a good chance we might want to check out the Shopaholics Anonymous meetings."

Madison's joke is aimed to make me feel better, but even though I smile, I can't get over the conflicting sides of the battle in my mind. Why do I so badly want to hop on the subway over to his place? Didn't I decide to leave because I need to go back to the life I already have but with a new perspective on things? Why couldn't I just stay here for the next couple of weeks? What am I going to do when I go back home and he's not within the same zip code as me?

I can't seem to look at her, so I start to fold clothes as I voice my inner conflict. "You know, after we talked last night and all the way to the point where I walked into the park, I had all of my answers. I didn't have any questions apart from wondering how the conversation would go and how he would react to it."

"And now?" she pushes.

"And now I'm not so sure I have it all figured out. One part of me knows that I have to leave and figure out how to deal with everything back at home. Then there's this other part of me that suddenly just wants to stay here and figure out how to bring that life here and make it new. None of this was here earlier. Now I'm filled with doubt and confusion. I'd really like confusion to be a person so I could punch him in the face right now."

We fold in silence for a few minutes as Madison either figures out how to respond, or waits to see if I'm going to add more. Either way, the only sound in the room is the two of us working on putting my clothes in the two rather large suitcases I brought with me. When I can no longer stand the thoughts dueling for the right to occupy my focus, I ask her what she thinks about the situation.

"I don't know, sweetheart. This is one of those times when it's all about you. Only you can figure out what's best for you." She puts the final clothes in the suitcase in front of her as I start to zip the other one up. "I know it seems hard right now, but when you sit down and really think about everything, you'll know what needs to be done."

God damn it. She's right again. I'll think about that later. After zipping up the other suitcase, we both lug them out of the room and towards the door. We roll the luggage to the elevator and I turn towards her to throw my arms out for her to fall into. We hold each other tightly in a hug even though we both know that she's going to be home for Christmas in a few weeks. It'll be different when we don't have each other in the next room to help with anything and everything.

"Thank you for letting me stay here," I say. "This stay was more than I could have ever asked for."

She pulls out of the hug. "Of course! I'm glad you came to stay. I think it was what you needed. Life is crazy and sometimes you need to do big things to change even the smallest aspects of your life."

We hear the ding of the elevator as the doors open. I roll bag one and then bag two into the elevator. I reach out to hug her again. She has me promise to text her when I get home to know that I got home safe. What a maternal thing to say. After promising her that I would do just that, I get in and press the button for the bottom floor. When I reach the lobby, I struggle to get my bags out. I need to remember to pack lighter next time. I walk out to the street and hail yet another cab. I place my bags in the trunk and say I'm going to JFK.

I situate myself before rummaging through my bag for my means of solace. My fingers find the cold silver and I put the buds in my ears. I know exactly who I want to be listening to right now. The music leaks into me and I allow myself to think about my feelings. As Paolo Nutini croons in my ears, I understand that there are a few things that I do know. Do I love Kiernan? Absolutely. Should I be going back to Indiana? Yes. Am I the better for coming here and, more importantly, having met him? Without a doubt. Can I go back and tackle college while embracing the unknown aspects of my future? There's nothing in the world that can hold me back anymore.

But what about the relationship aspect of my life? What about that? Once the period of non-communication ends between the two of us, there's a good chance that something might happen. As we exit Manhattan and it becomes background landscape, I come to the conclusion that yes, we were indeed supposed to meet. As it so happens, my iPod seems to agree.

I was so stranded
I was lost and abandoned
I needed another home
And you flew in my arms
You just flew right into my arms

I can't help but feel the words to the song are completely applicable to my situation. Let's not get it twisted, though. I don't believe in fate or serendipity or whatever else Hollywood is falsely perpetuating these days, but I do know that sometimes people fall into your life because they have to. Your life wouldn't make sense or be going in the right direction if they didn't. He helped pull me back to the real world and find all the things that I thought I had lost. The odd sensation of a hopeless romantic blossoming inside of me has me smiling and hoping that maybe one day, when we're both laying the roots down in our own ideas of Wonderland, we can hit up Home Depot for lumber to build our white picket fence.

The End

ACKNOWLEDGMENTS

There are quite a few people who deserve the credit for helping me spin this little tale of mine. Obviously I have to thank my parents for having me and never discouraging me from handing over a great deal of my money to many book venders. My brother and sister for allowing me to be the sibling that went into the arts. As the dedication shows, I have to thank Ben Horowitz for being incredibly helpful, supportive and encouraging. Megan Krueger deserves so much more than a thank you for being so patient and helpful throughout this entire process. I apologize for that bucket of crazy and side of raised voices I served you. Molly Sliwa, Kylie Morris, Aleksandra Coric, Marisa Meneghetti, Sarah Standley, Michelle Philipsborn, Jenny Eskander, Haley Barfoot and (the only dudes) Rob Hansen and Ben De Leon for reading whatever I scribbled out and giving me feedback. You're all amazing and deserve a cupcake. I have to thank the lovely Sara Harvey for editing this and being so wonderful. The amazing staff at AuthorHouse for allowing me the opportunity to have my story told. The two most important teachers I will ever have, Michelle Duffy and Jonas Wertin, deserve more than a thank you. New York City deserves a massive thank you for providing the perfect playground to place my story in. Chloe Witter for helping me find the right title. I could list a number of artists that provided inspiration but the two that deserve the most credit are The Avett Brothers and, most importantly, Jason Mraz. This book would never have started without "Plane" and the entire *Mr. A-Z* album. Lastly, I would like to thank *you* for purchasing this book. If you ever see me on the street and tell me you actually read this page, I will hug you. Thank you!

(I know I probably forgot a lot of people. I'm sorry. Don't worry, I still love you.)

Megan Mann

LaVergne, TN USA
27 October 2010

202370LV00001B/61/P